A Christmas Bonus

I0517519

EM Lynley

A CHRISTMAS BONUS

BY EM LYNLEY

Contents

EM Lynley

A CHRISTMAS BONUS

BY

EM LYNLEY

CHAPTER ONE

Monday, December 20
New York City

In five minutes Alec Compton would discover his fate.

He glanced at his watch and tried to swallow but his throat was dry as the martini he was already imagining, assuming the meeting went as planned.

Nearly Christmas, this was Alec's favorite time of year: bonus time at the Wall Street investment firm of Whitman, Whitman, and Walker—Three Dub to the Street—where he was a whisper away from making partner. They wouldn't distribute bonus checks until January, but at the obligatory pre-Christmas meeting with the firm's founding partners, he'd get a taste of what was in store.

He'd had a stellar year, his best yet, and he expected not only a healthy bonus but the long-awaited promotion to junior partner as well. Generally, the holiday mood of the whole office would be loud and bright, with admin staff wearing tinsel or shiny bows in their hair. This year had been tough given the state of the economy and markets, so nearly everyone was in a sour mood and there was nary a Santa hat in sight.

A few brave souls had hung gold or green garlands around their cubicles, but no one with an office had dared to decorate. The firm as a whole hadn't done well, and an office pool was already underway to guess which employees wouldn't be back after Christmas; a few people had already been let go, further depressing the already dismal holiday mood.

Alec couldn't delay reporting for his own assessment meeting any longer so he hauled himself out of his chair, pulled on his suit jacket, shot his cuffs, and headed for his boss's office. He moved silently but purposefully down the carpeted hall, and his colleagues nodded greetings as he passed open-door offices. The hallway was strung here and there with a few random Christmas decorations, and anemic sprigs of mistletoe hanging above a couple of doorways.

At the end of the long hall, he entered Ben Whitman's outer office. Gina Ravenna, Whitman's secretary, greeted him with a silent thumbs-up and a nod in the direction of the dark walnut door, slightly ajar. Alec took a deep breath and pushed it open.

Inside, Ben Whitman sat at a conference table so shiny the glare nearly blinded Alec. Flanking him were the other two founding partners: his younger brother Will Whitman, and Rob Walker, both looking more like the Grim Reaper than Santa's helpers.

Alec padded across the thick oriental carpet, hoping to straddle the line between cheerful optimism and somber acknowledgement of the firm's less-than-stellar results. He greeted the men with a tentative smile as he took a seat across table from them.

Usually he detected the aroma of contraband Cuban cigars, but this year, he barely noticed the scent of pine from the wreath behind Gina's desk. He dialed his smile back another notch.

Ben Whitman was known as "Big Ben" to Wall Street and the firm's employees, but never to his face. Alec and Ben had never really clicked. Despite Alec being considered the foremost up-and-coming star of the firm, Ben remained cool and distant toward him. Without so much as a greeting, Big Ben slid a yellow craft-paper envelope across the smooth, wide table, and left it sitting in the vast expanse halfway between himself and Alec.

Alec stared down at the envelope for a moment. He could see the reflection of the coffered ceiling in the highly polished mahogany. He glanced at Big Ben's face, its pale watery blue eyes betraying no emotion.

Alec waited for instructions.

"Open it up, Compton."

Alec turned the envelope over. His name was scrawled in spidery ink. The envelope felt light, giving Alec a little surge of relief. If they were cutting him loose, it would contain a thick sheaf of paperwork for him to sign, giving up his right to just about everything and anything he'd known or enjoyed while here at Three Dub. It must be a preview of his bonus check, which even with the firm's bad year, couldn't be too light. He resisted the urge to hold the envelope up to the Tiffany lamp a few feet away to see what it held before opening it.

With a dry mouth, Alec slipped a finger under the flap and eased it open. It was empty. He blinked a couple of times and peered inside again.

"Nothing in there but air, Compton. A little bit like some of our staff this past year."

Big Ben glanced over at his brother and the two of them chuckled.

Sure, let them yuk it up. Alec admitted to being surprised either of the Whitmans could even laugh; it was the first time he'd heard them express mirth.

"Schrader was in here just before you. *His* envelope had a big fat termination package." Big Ben paused for effect.

Alec tried to hold back a gasp, but a tiny strangled sound managed to escape. Schrader was *his* boss. If Schrader had gotten canned…

"Hank Schrader failed to close on the biggest deal we've even attempted here at Whitman, Whitman, and Walker." He never called the firm "Three Dub" or used any industry nicknames. The man was uptight formality to the bone. "So we're hoping you can step up to the plate and salvage the mess he's made."

He pronounced 'hoping' as if he really expected Alec to walk the plank and leap into a pool of starving sharks. About par for Wall Street.

Schrader had lost the Turner Foods deal? The one with Brant Linton as primary investor? Hank had been crowing for weeks, boasting he had Linton wrapped up like a fucking early Christmas present. Apparently Schrader had been drinking his own Kool-Aid and he'd OD'd on it before he'd actually accomplished his mission.

"We need the Turner Foods deal closed by December 31. If you succeed, you can have Schrader's bonus on top of what you've already earned this year. How does twice last year's bonus sound?"

"It sounds great."

"So you have two choices right now, Compton. You can have a big fat envelope like Schrader, or you can have a nice thin envelope with a big fat bonus check."

Alec knew which one he'd rather have. He looked Whitman in the eye. "I'll take door number two."

"Then what are you doing still sitting here? The clock is ticking." Whitman's face held no trace of amusement. He reached for the empty envelope and flapped it, then slid it back across the smooth, shiny. "A little reminder."

The envelope went flying off the table and onto the floor. Alec bent to pick it up, then exited deliberately, but not particularly quickly out of the room. He wouldn't let them see him run. But as soon as the door closed behind him, he raced back down the hall to his own office, slammed the door, and settled behind his desk. He stared at the empty envelope for a moment while he waited for his pulse to slow.

If he failed, he wouldn't get any bonus at all, which meant a year of hard work, twenty-hour days and working nearly every weekend would amount to nothing except an unemployment check. Even with a list of successful deals behind him, finding another position this lucrative would be difficult.

"I don't need no stinkin' reminder," he practically growled, crumpling the envelope and tossing it against the door. Time to see how he could possibly salvage the deal Schrader had started. The clock was ticking toward the deadline and time wasn't on his side.

He accessed the Turner files on the server and familiarized himself with the terms of the deal. Turner Foods, a conglomerate comprised of several smaller companies, manufactured and sold dozens, if not hundreds, of household names. Started as a family business over a hundred years earlier, it had expanded, but not always to the benefit of the bottom line.

Turner's management didn't appear to have much of a plan in mind when they added new products or divisions, and they were slow to cut their losses and discontinue unprofitable products. The firm had been foundering for years, failing to find new investors, and now the Turner leadership was ready to pack it in and sell to the highest bidder.

The prospective buyer was Linton Holdings, run by S. Brant Linton, considered the next Warren Buffet by the most respected business people, and featured regularly in the industry publications. Linton could easily turn the company's balance sheets around, after trimming away the fat and dismantling the core components, making Three Dub and another other investors a ton of money with nearly no risk.

Schrader had summed up the key benefits of the deal and Alec quickly got up to speed on the big picture. He'd dig into the details and the numbers later.

Working with Linton would be daunting, but it would be an incredible opportunity—as long as Alec had his shit together. No room for mistakes. Linton was known to be even more exacting than the top brass at Three Dub.

Alec rubbed his hands together and took a deep breath. He clicked on Linton's NY HQ phone number, and the computer dialed the number for him.

"Linton Holdings." The receptionist's voice managed to convey professionalism, competence, and helpfulness in just two words. Alec was suitably impressed.

"Brant Linton, please. This is Alec Compton from Whitman, Whitman, and Walker."

"One moment, Mr. Compton." Something about the receptionist's voice made Alec *want* to wait. Linton's team was top-notch all the way down to the admin staff.

To Alec's surprise, Brant Linton, rather than a secretary, answered after less than a minute. Alec was at a loss for words.

"Hello? Compton?" Brant sounded as professional as the operator, but instead of helpfulness, his voice held an edge of impatience.

"Mr. Linton, thanks for taking my call. I know how busy you are."

"Then get to the point."

Everything Alec had read about Linton was true. He didn't waste time with niceties. So neither would Alec.

"I'm calling to set up a time and place to close on the Turner Foods deal. I know you're interested, and we've got the rest of the funding in place. Can we can get the paperwork out of the way this week?"

"Refresh my memory on the terms."

Alec gave the shortest summary he could mentioning exact figures, deadlines and expected rates of return.

"Right, Compton. I'm about to step into a meeting. Call me back at six and I'll let you know where we stand."

"Okay and—" Beeps indicating the call had been terminated cut off the rest of Alec's words, and he slammed his own receiver down.

At two minutes to six he dialed Linton back.

"Compton, right on time. Good." Linton paused but started speaking again before Alec managed to get a greeting in edgewise. "I reread the details and there are two points which don't work for me. Specifically, to commit, I'm going to need...."

For the next several minutes, Linton concisely laid out his terms. Alec struggled to take sufficiently detailed notes. Thankfully they recorded all phone calls.

"I'll bring this up with the Turner management and get back to you with their decision," Alec said.

"Don't take too long."

"No, sir."

"Bring me the revised pitch book tomorrow by noon, including everything I just mentioned."

Alec heard the beeps again. Of course he wouldn't take too long. He had ten days until his number was up.

He couldn't let that happen.

He listened to the recorded call with Linton, went over his notes again, and considered how to proceed with Turner.

Then he grabbed the phone and called Marcus Hudson, one of the second-year associates. "Get your ass in here five minutes ago," Alec barked and hung up.

He watched the seconds tick by on his watch: 25 seconds later Marcus flew through the door and closed it behind him.

"Where would you like it?" Marcus asked as he clicked the door locked.

Alec blinked a couple of times until he realized what Marcus was talking about. Months ago there had been one very late night they'd been alone in the office and in the excitement and relief of getting a project done on time they'd, well, they hadn't been particularly professional, and afterward, Alec acted as if it hadn't happened. Technically he could get in serious trouble, no matter how willing Marcus had been. Marcus had hung off Alec's every word for a week or two, then resigned himself to their further interactions remaining strictly business.

Apparently, Marcus was still willing and eager for another go-round.

"I need you to build a new pitch book on the Turner-Linton deal for tomorrow." It was eight o'clock at night, though no first or second-year in their right mind would mention this fact, but Alec waited to see how Marcus would react.

"Can I get help?"

"Sure. Who's still here?"

"Everyone." Marcus's tone indicated it was a stupid question.

Alec smiled. Where else would everyone be at eight? The associates were always here until all the principals and partners left, just in case a director or partner needed help. No one wanted to be MIA when someone in power came looking for him. And no associate wanted to miss out on a chance for a great deal, and let one of his peers get the glory—and the bonus that went with all successful deals. Alec had played that game when he'd first started out, and he'd been both pushy and lucky to get a series of high-profile and highly profitable deals which got him noticed by Big Ben.

"Take two interns or first years, and start working. I'll email you the docs you'll need as I revise them. If you have any questions, call me, no matter the time. Don't assume anything and don't make any decisions on your own."

"But—"

"No exceptions and no buts on this."

Marcus cracked a smile, then it melted away when he realized Alec wasn't in a joking mood. "What's the deal?"

"Check your email." Alec nodded slightly in the direction of the door, dismissing Marcus. He knew Marcus was already running back to his desk, waiting for the little icon to pop up telling him a new email had arrived. Well, he could wait a few more minutes.

Alec picked up the phone and dialed Big Ben.

"I've got Linton back on the Turner buyout. I'll be taking him an expanded pitch book tomorrow, and I've got a team already on it."

Alec wasn't sure exactly what he'd expected Whitman to say, but the only response he got was, "Be in my office with the book by nine a.m."

"Okay—" *Beep, beep, beep.* He'd already hung up.

Alec looked up at the ceiling and let out a very long sigh. Nothing ever changes. Everyone craps on the person below them on the totem pole. He'd done it to Marcus and as soon as Marcus got the email, he'd start crapping on whichever two unfortunates he chose for his team.

No matter, Alec mused. He was already adding up how much dry cleaning that big fat bonus check would buy.

CHAPTER TWO

"I've got the new pitch book ready for you. When should I drop it off?" Alec held his breath as he waited for Linton to respond. Maybe his tone was slightly too aggressive with someone of Linton's stature, but the gamble usually paid off. The Turner buyout would make Linton a packet; he wasn't likely to change his mind and miss out on the profit just because Alec didn't kiss his ass.

Not that Alec would mind kissing Linton's ass or any other part of him, literally. For the fiftieth time he flipped through the recent photo spread and interview in *Forbes*. Times had really changed on Wall Street even before Apple's CEO Tim Cook came out, and the magazine had made strides to portray the few openly gay execs with dignity and sensitivity. They'd also named S. Brant Linton as one of the top ten most eligible gay businessmen in America.

And how.

Alec would be the first to admit he'd drooled over the man in the photos. At age thirty-nine, Linton wasn't just handsome, he was distinguished. His dark hair had a sprinkling of silver strands just making an appearance at his temples and in his sideburns.

"Can you get here in thirty minutes?"

Alec pulled himself back to reality. "Sure. Be right there." He shoveled papers into a briefcase, and then ran to the men's room to make sure he looked presentable before he headed out.

Once out on the street, a December breeze stung his ears and made his eyes tear. He watched his breath bloom into a hazy nebula as he exhaled. Damn it was going to be a cold winter. He'd been considering a ski trip in Switzerland, but vacation wasn't an option till January now, *if* he closed this deal. If he didn't, Big Ben would be giving him the opportunity for a very extended vacation. Unpaid.

He flagged down a taxi in nothing flat, and for once traffic wasn't snarled into immobility as he traveled uptown. Good thing a lot of people had already headed out for the holidays.

In less than fifteen minutes, Alec exited the taxi in front of the Chrysler building, where Linton Holdings' offices occupied two floors. The downstairs lobby's interior mirrored the building's exterior, with rich period furnishings and smooth, honey-colored wood paneling and original artwork on the walls.

"Mr. Linton is running late, but you can go in and wait in his office," the charming blond woman in Linton's outer office told Alec when he approached her Art Deco desk. She wore an elegant black and white silk blouse, and her smooth chignon reminded Alec of a '40s-era film star. Bright red lipstick completed the image. The dramatic look worked on her and she complemented the décor perfectly.

Alec seated himself across from the smooth, sexy curves of the polished cherry wood desk and waited. Linton had told him to be here in thirty minutes, but twenty-five minutes later, no Linton. Probably some sort of test. Linton's reputation for making people jump through hoops was well known and clearly well deserved.

Instead of stewing or shuffling his feet, Alec got up and wandered around the beautiful office. It wasn't the incredible view of Manhattan below, encompassing the UN

Headquarters building, the snow-covered Roosevelt Island or the far shore of the East River across the river that caught Alec's attention.

What he wanted to discover was what kind of *man* Brant Linton was, not what kind of businessman.

Linton's desk was clear except for the sleek and spare Mac, which looked as good as any sculpture, and a grouping of framed photographs clustered in one corner, all facing Linton. Unlike Linton's peers, his walls didn't display his diplomas or honorary doctorates. Alec recalled from articles he'd read that Linton hadn't attended business school; he'd been mentored by Byron Voight, one of the older generation of buy-out kings, though Linton had since been awarded numerous honorary business degrees.

Instead of displaying such trappings of status or achievement, one wall held several museum-quality paintings, undoubtedly originals. Alec moved in for a closer look at one which caught his attention. He knew immediately from the style it had been painted by Gauguin. While the artist's most famous work featured native island women, this one depicted a male nude on a white beach, with blue-hued hill, and a lavender sky in the background. The textured brushwork, and the masterful command of color and depth fascinated him. He'd never seen a Gauguin quite this close before, even in a museum.

How must it feel to own something this valuable and important, to be able to look at and touch whenever you wanted? He reached a finger toward the surface, aching to caress the distinctive raised brushwork. Linton would never know, but Alec had more respect for the painting and pulled his hand back.

Someday, he promised himself. *Someday I'll own something this incredible, this important.* He tore himself away from the painting, quickly glancing toward the door, lest Linton to show up while he was coveting the man's possessions and position.

On the opposite wall hung a series of photos, only one of which showed Linton with someone Alec recognized: three of the last four presidents. But what really caught Alec's attention were the personal photos on the desk. They were arranged so only Linton could see them while seated at his desk. Alec slipped behind the desk and faced the door, so he would be able to hear or see Linton before he entered, so he took the chance and picked up one of the framed photos.

The largest showed Linton—shirtless, tanned and very well-muscled, making Alec need to fan himself a bit—standing with a shorter, sandy-haired slightly stocky man and a striking dark-haired woman on a high-masted sailboat. Linton's dark wavy hair was windblown, giving him a carefree, almost wild look that suited him as well as his more usual tailored business attire. Two little kids, maybe five or six years old, flanked the adults, and everyone wore wide natural smiles, signifying genuine enjoyment.

The photo jogged Alec's memory about the *Forbes* article: Linton's sister Eleanor lived with her chef husband and their twins somewhere in French Polynesia not far from Tahiti.

Painted on the stern of the pictured boat was its name: *Premiere Cru*, Taha'a. The name struck Alec, because it sounded like something a French chef or a billionaire American businessman might name a boat.

"Compton?"

The voice boomed from behind Alec, startling him, and he dropped the frame with a resounding crash onto the desk, knocking over several other photos, domino-style. Alec swore under his breath and whirled around to see Brant Linton enter the room through an almost-invisible side entrance to the office, reminiscent of the one depicted in photographs of the Oval Office. Had Linton put one in here because it made him feel like the president?

Finally Alec stood face to face with the man he'd so far only read about. After the initial shock and embarrassment at being found fingering the man's belongings, the first thought to cross Alec's mind was how none of the photographs did Brant Linton justice. Tall and handsome in a rugged and distinguished way, his intelligent, thoughtful green eyes twinkled with what could be amusement or mischief, not the rebuke Alec had undoubtedly earned.

To make matters worse, Alec discovered not only was he most likely blushing with some of decidedly unprofessional thoughts about Linton, but that blood had also rushed south of the border. His unprofessional interest might soon become embarrassingly obvious.

Belatedly, Alec recalled the frames he'd knocked over on the desk and reached to straighten them, his hand bumping into

Linton's as he also reached for the displaced photographs.

* * * *

"Have a seat." Brant took the photo and motioned toward the chair facing the desk as he watched Alec Compton attempt to recover his poise. He tried not to grin at the effect he'd had on his unsuspecting visitor as he seated himself in his comfortable leather armchair and continued to observe his victim.

Compton still held one frame in his hand and reached out to put it on the desk. Brant leaned forward to take the photo, and his fingers momentarily brushed against Compton's. He hadn't been prepared for the high-voltage shock from that briefest of contact, and it distracted him as he attempted to gather his thoughts.

"My card." Alec Compton pulled a thin gold card case out of his inner jacket pocket, and the suit's label came into view: D&G, on the daring side for a banker, but Compton wore it well. The man knew his clothing, and made a wise choice in a suit that accentuated his tall, slender frame. Brant took the card, letting their fingers touch again—less accidentally and far more pleasurably. He put the card on his desk without looking at it as Compton continued.

"Mr. Linton, I've got—"

"Brant, please." He liked the way Alec's eyes lit up at the informality, but it would be a mistake to get too casual too quickly. Compton was here to work, not play, and despite what that recent *Forbes* article had said, Brant wasn't exactly single. Not that he advertised his relationship. He'd let the journalist believe he was a bachelor, and he didn't have any photos of AK here in the office.

It was only at this moment, Brant fully realized that omission. He glanced at the frames he did have: all of his sister Ellie and her family, except for one or two of happy childhood times.

"—the details, but the deal contains all the elements you and Hank Schrader previously discussed."

Alec Compton had been talking and Brant had been staring at him and daydreaming. A bad combination. He'd never seen eyes like Alec's—deep gray irises with an irregular halo of gold ringing the pupils. With immense effort he averted his gaze, letting it play along the painting Compton had come too close to touching. The excitement of his upcoming holiday trip had finally gotten to Brant. He was far too distracted to finalize a deal right now, especially one this big.

"Why isn't Schrader here?" Brant hadn't really liked Schrader, a puffy red-faced man who'd seemed to sweat constantly and belch at inopportune moments—such as in the middle of a sentence when everyone in the room had their attention focused on him. He'd always run late, and, even though Schrader's business skills were sharp as tacks, Brant had always felt something was missing.

Clearly someone at Three Dub thought he'd be more likely to finally sign on the dotted line if they sent over this young, attractive associate. Brant wasn't sure if he should be appreciative of the eye candy, or offended they were playing to his tastes. The situation was reminiscent of the way the old boys might suggest a night at a strip club or invite some pros to a private party.

"Hank's started his vacation early this year."

Smooth answer, Brant thought. He glanced down at the card: Alec Compton wasn't just an associate, he was a director, one level below partner. Despite his deceptively youthful appearance, thanks in part to thick, honey-brown locks, he'd impressed someone at his firm.

Let's see what he can do, and not make this too easy on him. Let him earn this deal if he's as good as he thinks he is.

"I want to look at your revisions and get back to you. But you should know, I'm not prepared to fully finance the deal at this point, even with the change in terms." Brant waited a beat to see how Compton would respond, and he wasn't disappointed.

"We've got counterparties already in place for twenty-five percent of the financing. I believe Hank had everything in place for some time."

Brant smiled. Compton was correct. Schrader had lined up the outside financing from Three Dub's existing clients. Less risk for Linton Holdings, but less profit, too, once he started dismantling Turner Foods. Time to wipe the grin off Compton's pretty face. "It's a go if you can bring in forty percent outside money."

Brant couldn't recall exactly why he'd put this deal on hold, and he needed time to check out the details in the pitch book. He rattled off a list of additional demands, most of which were petty requests and none of them deal breakers. But he wouldn't let Compton or Three Dub know that.

"Forty percent *and* those new terms?" Compton's confidence visibly wavered now.

Brant felt a surge of adrenalin as he watched Alec make quick mental calculations. Compton pursed his lips slightly, and a series of extremely unprofessional images crossed Brant's mind about that mouth. He shifted in his seat, feeling heat spreading between his legs.

The combination of Compton's presence and the thrill of doing a deal were almost more than he could handle at the moment. He felt only slightly guilty at his arousal at Compton's expense, but then again, he did hold all the cards. Compton, Three Dub, and their clients needed him and his millions, which was the way he liked it.

"Ben Whitman's hoping we could close this before the end of the year."

"That would be impressive. That gives you less than twenty-four hours to get your ducks lined up *and* all the paperwork ready for signatures." Not an insurmountable challenge. Brant knew plenty of bankers out there who'd give their left nut to be in on a deal with him.

He didn't have a perfect record, but his rate of return was significantly higher than his competitors', and a deal with him was almost a sure moneymaker for everyone involved.

He'd be surprised if Compton couldn't come up with financing for an additional fifteen percent of the asking price within twenty-four hours. Even Schrader could have managed that. But he doubted Turner would agree to the new conditions, so it would rest on Compton's ability to candy-coat the terms. If he pulled it off, he deserved to close the deal. And Brant could still delay if he wasn't happy once he reviewed the amended contracts.

"It's only December twentieth . . ." Compton said.

"True, but I'm heading for French Polynesia tomorrow night for my Christmas holiday. All family and no business. My sister —" Brant held up the photograph that had caught Compton's interest earlier. "—always complains when I visit that I'm on the phone half the time working one deal or another. This year I am determined not to bring business along. Either get me the final contract tomorrow, or we can continue this discussion in January."

Brant wasn't sure why he'd given so much information to Alec Compton. He found himself lulled into a comfortable familiarity with the attractive man sitting in front of him. He really needed a vacation or he'd start giving away profits as easily as personal details.

"Right. Tomorrow." Compton stood and turned toward the door.

"I'll look over the book tonight, but I'll expect your call when you've talked to Turner and lined up the additional funding." Without thinking Brant held out his card. "These are my direct numbers."

Alec pocketed the card, the excitement in his silver-and-gold eyes mirroring Brant's, though Brant couldn't explain his own reaction. He got pitched a dozen deals a week, so why did this one get his motor racing?

All he knew for sure was he wanted to see Alec Compton again. There couldn't be a worse reason for going ahead with the deal. Wrong in so many ways Brant didn't even want to contemplate.

The physical excitement didn't die down even after Compton departed. Brant flipped through the pitch book but couldn't concentrate on the figures and decided to call it a day. It would be nice to surprise AK by getting home early for a change. And AK would undoubtedly repay Brant with some much-needed physical release. He tossed the pitch book in his case and headed home, hoping some hot and heavy one-on-one time with AK would erase the images of Alec Compton still filling his brain.

CHAPTER THREE

It was only two in the afternoon when Alec left Linton's office. His heart raced and blood pounded through his body when Linton had walked in on him staring at those personal photos. Despite his experience and the preparation he'd done for the meeting, being caught like that had put Alec at a disadvantage. He simply hadn't been prepared for the effect meeting Brant Linton would have on him, and it had nothing to do with the deal.

Despite his reputation, Linton hadn't been stern or imposing. Instead he'd been so fucking hot Alec had barely been able to keep his mind on business. He'd felt a surge of physical attraction from the moment their fingers had brushed, and he'd had to use every ounce of concentration to keep his body from responding. Linton looked handsome and fit in the *Forbes* spread, but in person, he was captivating.

Alec had felt like a freshman with a crush on the professor as he sat in Linton's office,

EM Lynley

trying not to stare—or drool. And Linton had barely even looked at him. Only when he offered his private numbers had Alec felt— fleetingly—an electric tingle between them, but he'd brushed off the impression as the result of an overactive imagination and libido.

All the way back to the office Alec replayed their interactions. "He likes me, he likes me not," like a fucking junior high school girl chanting and pulling petals off a flower. But now Alec had even more motivation to line this deal up and get back into Linton's office, even if just to smell the man again.

He was still pretty worked up when he got back to Three Dub and passed Marcus in the hallway.

"Marcus, I need your help on the Linton project again," he barked at the associate who eagerly trailed into Alec's office.

"Shut the door... and lock it," he said once Marcus arrived, letting his tone communicate what he'd been thinking.

Marcus nodded his assent and loosened his tie, giving Alec a clear go-ahead.

This time, Alec barely hesitated before pulling Marcus close. Marcus opened his mouth and let Alec in.

But it wasn't Marcus that Alec wanted. And fucking the associates in his office wasn't a realistic or appropriate way to deal with the sexual tension spilling over from meeting Brant Linton. He stepped back and removed Marcus' hands from his body.

"I've got another assignment for you."

Disappointment visibly oozed from Marcus, but he nodded and listened to Alec's request, then left.

Ben Whitman was expecting to hear from Alec, so he straightened his clothing and headed for Big Ben's office to update him in person on the Linton deal.

Still needing physical release after that uncomfortable face-to-face, Alec decided a few quick miles at the executive gym on the sixteenth floor would do him a world of good and allow him to focus on work again.

It was only once he was back in his office, body only slightly more relaxed and mind again able to focus on the task at hand, that he went over Linton's new demands. In the rush of desire and excitement in Linton's office, Alec had simply scribbled the new terms on his pad without thinking them through. Now he understood what Linton wanted, it would be an even tougher song-and-dance to get Turner management to agree.

Turner's headquarters were in the Midwest, so the CEO, Steve Turner, should still be available at this time of day. Alec called and laid out Linton's revised offer. Linton was taking advantage of the combination of lessening demand for their products exacerbated by an overall economic downturn, give Alec serious qualms—and a conflict of interest—on this deal.

Turner Foods had been unwilling to make substantial changes to its product line while continuing to offer overly-generous compensation and retirement for their employees. Current management—the youngest generation of the Turner family— had little sentimental attachment to the product line, preferring to dump the company while it still had some value. Alec suspected they could get a better offer than Linton's, and he was torn between getting the best price for the company and saving his own ass. He'd see how Turner responded to the tender before offering advice.

But Steve Turner practically jumped at Linton's new terms and Alec kept his own concerns to himself. Turner was happy, which made Alec (and the Dubs) happy. He'd get a healthy bonus on this deal, and lock in that promotion. Being the first at Three Dub to close a deal with Brant Linton should be more than enough to merit a junior partnership. Not even the founding partners had managed to hook him for anything so far.

For the first time all day, Alec let himself relax, just a tiny bit.

For one indulgent minute he considered how he'd spend his bonus: a new car? A down payment on a nice co-op? A shopping trip to Italy? *Now we're talking.* He'd been dreaming of a trip to Northern Italy, and while he knew he'd enjoy every minute of the food, architecture, and fashion, it would be so much more enjoyable to experience Italy with someone special.

There hadn't been anyone in his life for far too long. With his insane work hours, aside from the extracurricular activities with Marcus, he'd only managed the occasional casual hook-up, none of whom he'd liked enough to meet a second time.

After years of blood, sweat, tears, and sacrifices in his personal life, his future here came down to this one deal. If he lost it, Alec would have fuck-all to show for his time at Three Dub.

He had a lot of ground to cover over the next twelve hours.

* * * *

The sun had already set when Brant climbed into the backseat of his chauffeur-driven vintage Jaguar for the ride home. He craved the buffer between work and home more than usual today, but even cracking the window to let in the frigid December air didn't cool him off enough after the brief exchange with Alec Compton.

He wondered how long it would take Compton to get back to him with the new contracts, then he chided himself for thinking more about Alec's mouth and the way his suit hugged his body than about the deal. He wasn't single anymore and cheating was against his rules.

"Stop at that florist up on the next corner," he instructed the driver, then hopped out to purchase a medium-sized bouquet of bright tropical flowers for AK. Too big and AK would suspect Brant's real reason for the impromptu gift.

Arriving home hours earlier than usual, Brant unlocked the door to his penthouse. He stepped inside, and flipped on the light switch with an elbow, his attention focused on the bundle of mail Oleg, the front-desk clerk, had handed him.

"AK, would you believe I'm home already?" He dropped his keys into the crystal bowl on the stand near the door, but instead of the familiar clink, the keys plummeted with a dull thud on the thick hall carpeting.

The crystal bowl was gone, along with the antique chest on which it had sat when Brant had left the apartment that morning. He blinked a few times, then dropped the day's mail on the floor and headed deeper into the apartment with the bouquet.

"AK? Alaska?" Brant used the nickname that had sprung naturally from the initials.

No answer, and Brant soon discovered why. The little stand by the door wasn't the only thing missing; half his living room furniture was gone.

Brant stood in the middle of the room, clutching the flowers and surveyed his surroundings.

Where was AK and why had he taken the furniture? *When* had he taken it? Brant thought everything had been there that morning, but he barely glanced up most mornings as he rushed to get to the office.

He typically left in the pre-dawn darkness, arriving in the office early enough to talk with Europe before the US markets opened, then stayed until Hong Kong opened, meaning at least till seven or eight at night, often later if he was working a deal on a different continent. And half the time he was out of town on business of one sort or another.

Now, Brant went over to the bar—built in, so still there—and poured half a glass of Balvenie 21. He settled himself into one of the remaining chairs facing the floor-to-ceiling window and stared out into the velvet darkness over the twinkling Manhattan city lights.

He pulled his cell phone out of his pocket and called AK. From across the room, Brant heard a familiar sound: AK's disco-beat ring tone.

So he'd taken the furniture but left his phone? Brant didn't like games. At work he expected people to tell him the truth, whether it was good or not, and he'd deal with it.

But AK could never just *say* what he wanted. He expected Brant to read his mind, and when Brant couldn't, AK found ways to make his life difficult.

Maybe that was to be expected. AK was an actor. Or to hear him say it, an Ac*tor,* with much emphasis on the second syllable and most definitely capitalized. Despite his talent, he'd been having a hard time advancing his career beyond Off-Broadway productions, in part because he refused to play gay characters, no matter the role or the production.

"If I do, I'll end up being typecast from now on," he'd justified. Instead he chose roles that were as unlike his real personality as possible, and while he received overall decent reviews, he never earned the raves his talent deserved.

Brant had given up offering AK any advice about his career. Brant had plenty of experience of his own with trying to succeed as something he wasn't. For Brant, it hadn't been about being gay, but he'd tried for years to follow one path, and only after a horrible mistake, admitted he wasn't only hurting himself, but others. Once he'd found his niche, he'd excelled far beyond anything he'd ever hoped. But everyone had to discover their own path.

He took too large a swallow of the amber liquid and nearly choked. The port-barrel-aged whisky was meant to be sipped, savored, not gulped. But Brant craved the burn, the pain, and the Balvenie was too smooth and sophisticated. He noted how little remained in the bottle: clearly AK had enjoyed more than Brant had.

Was he was being too hard on AK?

He didn't mind giving AK anything within reason. All he wanted was some appreciation and understanding when he couldn't live his life on AK's terms or schedule.

Not that he hadn't wanted to give AK most anything he'd asked for, but there were limits.

They'd started off as a relationship of convenience on both sides: Brant wanted a good-looking companion on a strictly casual basis. AK had enjoyed Brant's company and his money, allowing him to enjoy a lifestyle far beyond his earnings. For a while in the middle they'd grown truly fond of each other, then Brant's brutal schedule combined with AK's demands for more time and everything began to unravel into ugliness.

In an effort to repair their crumbling relationship, Brant had invited AK to come along to spend Christmas in the islands with Ellie and her family

AK had been elated with the prospected of a trip to Taha'a, one of the most remote and exclusive—and therefore, expensive—islands in French Polynesia. He'd gone shopping for the kids' holiday gifts, new clothes for the trip, and even offered to pack for both of them.

AK wouldn't have missed the chance to hobnob with the royalty and celebrities who vacationed there for the world, or so Brant had thought.

But they'd quarreled again the previous night while packing for the trip, presumably prompting AK's escalation tactics today. His timing couldn't have been worse. They were scheduled to leave the following night for at least a week of sun, sand, and family.

As cold-hearted as it might sound, Brant questioned how much he'd actually miss AK. Because he genuinely enjoyed AK's company, and the usually mind-blowing sex, Brant had tried unsuccessfully to adapt. AK apparently had taken solace in what Brant could give him: a lot of zeroes in front of the decimal point.

That brought Brant back to here and now. He glanced at his watch—barely seven, but he was exhausted. He could run after AK, or he could move forward without him.

What he craved right now was a good night's sleep on his own schedule.

In the bedroom, Brant was relieved to find his two suitcases where they'd been that morning. AK's own suitcases were gone, along with everything from his side of the closet.

Brant sat down on the bed, unmade as usual, and sighed. No point in wasting time, he got up, carefully took off his suit and hung it up, then tossed shirt, socks, and underwear in the hamper. After washing up, he stepped back and took a good look at himself in the mirror.

He couldn't pinch an inch of belly fat, but he wasn't in particularly good shape. Not the shape he wanted to be in. Too many hours in the office, too much coffee and take-out, even from top restaurants, and not enough time sleeping or exercising.

January was nearly here, and he'd make a New Year's resolution to get to the gym more often, get some definition back in what had been a body he'd been proud of. Not that he wasn't a catch, at least according to that damn *Forbes* piece.

Top ten eligible gay businessmen. Someone out there would enjoy what he did have to offer.

He flipped off the bathroom light and headed back to the bedroom, this time grabbing his cell phone and emailing AK a short "Call me. Please." Normally not one to waste words, he'd added the "please" as an afterthought. Given the situation, he realized it was necessary.

Ten minutes later, Brant's cell chimed. *AK* flashed on the display.

"AK? Alaska?" Brant felt an unfamiliar catch in his throat. Suddenly, he didn't want things to end like this. Something in him wanted to give their relationship another chance. Maybe it was guilt over the misplaced physical reaction to Alec Compton. Or maybe it was just the warm holiday spirit that had infused him since that morning. He hadn't realized how much he'd been looking forward to the trip—needed it—and to seeing his sister and her family, revisiting cherished family memories and traditions.

"So, you noticed something was missing after all." AK's voice sounded unnaturally calm.

"Of course I noticed. Where are you, AK?"

"Does it even matter?"

"Of course it matters. I came home early just to see you." Brant's guilt-meter hit the red zone again, and he focused on picturing AK's face and not Alec's.

"So you thought about what we discussed last night?" A hopeful note brightened AK's voice.

AK's Christmas request was for Brant to back a show for him. Brant's gut churned. "Not really, but we can talk about it while we're away."

"How about if we talk about it now, before the trip?"

"Why is that suddenly the most important issue?"

"You know why, and if you don't, my telling you wouldn't fix it."

Brant thought this might be the most intelligent thing AK had ever said, summing up their entire relationship and how ill-suited they were for each other.

"Look, I know I've been particularly busy lately, but I hoped we'd have plenty of time to make up over the holiday, on the island." Brant waited, knowing exactly was going through AK's mind. He'd been less interested in Brant's family than in the chance to visit the exclusive resort at the other end of the island.

"Brant, maybe we need some time just the two of us. Could you postpone the trip a day or two?"

"It's only a few days before Christmas. Postponing doesn't leave much time to spend with the kids."

"Please?"

"This trip is for both of us."

"If you really cared about us . . . about *me* . . ."

The whine in that last syllable was unmistakable.

AK had long since crossed the border into outright manipulation, and Brant had had it. He was finished with this conversation and with AK. He would never let someone treat him like this on a deal, and he'd given AK far too much for the relationship to rest on a last-minute stunt.

"Merry Christmas, AK." Brant snapped his phone shut, turned off the ringer, and put it on the nightstand with a surprising sense of relief and satisfaction.

"Merry Christmas, Brant," he said out loud and wondered why it had taken this long to give himself this gift. "You are now officially single—and officially on vacation."

Time to escape the usual stress and expectations, to spend time with people who didn't want something from him 24/7. He was already packed, and with AK out of the picture of his own volition there was no reason not to start his Christmas holiday a little bit early. He'd head out first thing in the morning for Ellie's instead of waiting another day. Nothing that couldn't wait until he got back from paradise, right?

He slipped under the covers, turned off the light and fell almost immediately into a welcome and untroubled sleep.

He slept deliciously late and it was nearly eight when he finally woke up alone and more refreshed than he could remember. The empty bed only reinforced his decision.

While nibbling on buttered toast, Brant phoned his pilot to prepare for immediate departure. Then he called Maxine, his assistant, and told her to send everyone home—with their bonus envelopes and full pay—until January 3. Her joyful laughter told him he'd made the correct decision.

"If anyone has an emergency, tell 'em to come find me in Taha'a, but it better be life or death."

CHAPTER FOUR

Alec Compton worked late into the night, and started early the next morning calling a list of clients who were so eager to participate in a deal with Three Dub and Linton Holdings, he could have come up with 75 percent of the final figure if Linton had wanted.

Meanwhile, Marcus worked with Legal to draft new contracts for Big Ben to approve before Alec delivered them to Linton. There would be minor changes here and there, but Alec suspected Linton's handshake should be enough for Big Ben. Then Alec could consider the deal a fait accompli and earn a bonus check instead of a pink slip.

Alec arrived at Linton HQ with time to spare for his noon meeting. After being up all night, he'd managed to sneak home for a shower and change of clothes. He wanted to look fresh and presentable for Linton, not like he'd been working his ass off since he'd left the office the day before. That's what Linton expected, but Alec wouldn't give him the satisfaction.

Of course, he wanted to look good just for Brant Linton, regardless—and he was certainly open to other forms of satisfaction, if the opportunity presented itself. He smiled at the way his body heated up at the prospect, and forced himself to calm down. Once Linton signed onto this deal Alec could expect to spend plenty of time hammering out the—uh, details—in the months ahead.

As Alec practically floated down the hall toward Linton's office, he noticed people carrying presents and laptops, as though already finishing up before the holiday, though it was still several days before Christmas.

Some investment firms wouldn't even let employees leave early on Christmas Eve, but Linton's people were clustered in chatty little groups, sipping champagne, and more than a few hummed Christmas songs as they made their way toward the elevator.

Must be bonus day already here at Linton Holdings, which reminded Alec of his own predicament, and he moved more quickly down the hall to Linton's office.

"I'm sorry, Mr. Compton, but Mr. Linton's already gone for the holidays." The blonde bombshell assistant smiled at him as she hurriedly set her own glass of champagne down on the desk out of sight.

Alec didn't need to utter a word; clearly his expression told the woman everything.

"I am so sorry about this. He called first thing this morning and told everyone to go home until January. I'm just here rescheduling all his appointments and then I'm out the door." She glanced up at him. "Did you say you had a noon appointment today? You're not on his sche— Oh, here you are on the *private* calendar." She bit her lower lip. "I forgot to remind him of your meeting before he left."

Private calendar? On any other day that would have been flattering. But not when he was standing here and Brant Linton was already gone for the rest of the goddamned year.

"I'll put you on his calendar for Monday, January third at nine in the morning, so you will be absolutely first on his list after he returns."

What a fucking disaster! Alec's guts twisted in on themselves, but he forced himself to smile and sputtered out a more businesslike response. "Is there any way to get in touch with him before then?"

"Only upon pain of death. He's visiting his sister and her kids near Tahiti, and he gave very strict instructions. Honestly, it's not worth my job to disobey those orders." She gave a cheerful laugh, perhaps not completely joking. "He told me if it was a life-or-death emergency, you're welcome to go find him over there yourself."

Alec barely paid attention to her as he started to turn away. "Thanks, and Merry Christmas or Happy Chanukah, or whatever you celebrate."

"Thanks, Mr. Compton. Same to you and your family." She picked up the glass of champagne she'd hidden behind a stack of books on her desk and gave him a symbolic toast before sipping.

Yeah, my family. Given his ridiculous work schedule, Three Dub was the closest Alec *had* to a family at the moment, and only if you were into backstabbing control freaks. So much for the holiday spirit.

But Brant Linton *was* into family. Alec racked his brain to remember the photograph he'd seen on Linton's desk. Once Linton had shown up, Alec had focused his attention on ogling the man while not embarrassing himself, but one photo remained seared into his brain: Linton with his sister and kids on that gorgeous sailboat. The same one pictured in the magazine article. *Premiere Cru,* out of Taha'a.

Alec gave a satisfied nod as the secretary's words sunk into his consciousness. This was a life-or-death emergency, wasn't it? No doubt that Alec's death was imminent if Big Ben heard he'd let Linton leave the fucking *continent* without signing.

Brant Linton and Taha'a, here I come!

Twenty minutes later Alec's good mood had fizzled faster than a bottle of cheap New York sparkling wine. Stuck in traffic in a cab on the way back to his office, he'd tried to book a plane ticket, only to discover there was no airport on Taha'a and no flights available to Raiatea, the closest island with an airport.

He couldn't even find a package vacation or hotel room on any of the islands. Everything was booked solid for two months, even at the most expensive resorts. He couldn't remember the last time he used a real-live travel agent, so he called Big Ben's secretary as the cab inched along on one of the few remaining shopping days before Christmas.

"Help me, Gina. I need to get to Taha'a to see Brant Linton. Do you know a good travel agent who might be able to help me find a flight and hotel?"

"Hang on just a sec ...." Alec could hear her perfectly polished acrylic nails clacking away at the keyboard. "Just emailed you the contact info for Carmella Parigi. Good luck. And pack sunscreen. Make sure to eat plenty of lobster and fresh fish for me like the Bachelorette did."

"What bachelorette?"

"You know, the TV show. They filmed one season on that island. Absolute paradise!"

"Thanks, Gina, I owe you one."

"More than one, sugar, but I'm still hoping you change teams so you can pay me back properly."

He laughed and disconnected.

Even Gina's travel agent pal couldn't get him any closer than Bora Bora, still a few islands away from Taha'a. She suggested hiring a boat to travel between islands once he arrived, so he booked a flight leaving late that evening—at an exorbitant price he'd eat if he lost the deal—and directed the cab toward home so he could pack.

CHAPTER FIVE

Wednesday, December 22
Above Raiatea, French Polynesia

"We'll be landing in half an hour," Michelle, the sole member of the luxurious G-IV's cabin crew, informed Brant Linton. She handed him a warm towel and a placed a glass of iced water on the table next to him.

"Thanks." Brant wiped his face and hands, freshening up after a short nap, then gulping most of the refreshing liquid.

He'd spent most of the trip emailing or talking with one of his attorneys, whom he'd instructed to determine the value of property AK had removed from the apartment. If it exceeded a particular—and quite generous—amount, the attorney was prepared to initiate legal proceedings. Otherwise, Brant considered the matter closed.

He arranged for locks to be changed as necessary, and for all staff to refuse entrance to AK if he returned while Brant was away. Owning the entire building made dealing with issues like this simple.

He moved to a window seat and stared out at the expanse of smooth turquoise ocean, broken only by the occasional foamy swell or the golden sun glinting off the surface. In the distance, he spotted land.

Butterflies jostled in his stomach as he let the excitement of travel take over, replacing the stress of the business he'd handled on board. He couldn't remember the last time he'd traveled that *hadn't* been for business. Even the few trips he and AK had taken had been to close one deal or another. AK had come along with Brant; only to find himself exploring an exotic, enchanted destination alone while Brant stayed indoors for meetings and negotiations often lasting into the wee hours of the morning.

Brant knew he worked himself too hard to enjoy the pleasures and luxuries his wealth afforded. Well, no more. During this trip he planned to let loose and have some real fun for a change. He hadn't seen Ellie's kids, twins, just like he and Ellie, for a couple of years, and it had been much longer since he'd been to the island.

Ellie and her chef husband Henri had moved to Taha'a when the twins were still crawling, and the now her family considered it home. Located in the south Pacific, Taha'a was part of French Polynesia, near Tahiti, but much farther off the beaten path. It had managed to remain all but unknown to travelers and vacationers, except for the wealthiest, and that was how the locals preferred it.

Now Taha'a was home to some of the most exclusive resorts in the universe. Ellie joked it was easier to get a flight on the space shuttle than to get into either of Taha'a's opulent resorts unless you knew someone who knew someone who knew royalty.

The status quo had changed only slightly after a reality TV show had visited to film several episodes, and the few rooms at the more affordable resort were booked up for the next three years. The smaller resort, with only twelve private bungalows, didn't even take reservations from the public.

The rest of the island continued almost blissfully immune from tourism, its economy centered on pearl cultivation and vanilla farming. There were few amenities for outsiders, so when Brant visited, family was first and foremost.

Unless he was working on a deal. But he wasn't this time. Still, he took his last few moments of relative freedom to glance over his investments and standing orders with the necessary brokers, so he wouldn't be tempted to monitor movements in the financial markets during his visit.

"Fasten your seatbelt, sir," pilot Tuck Wilbur, announced from the cockpit, and five minutes later the nimble plane touched down so smoothly the ice barely clinked in Brant's glass.

The plane halted at the small terminal on Raiatea, Taha'a's neighbor and nearest airport. Tuck exited the cabin and stood next to his wife, Michelle, then saluted Brant in an overly formal style, a holdover from Tuck's military days.

"Great flight, Tuck. You two are welcome to either stay in the islands or head home if you prefer to spend the holidays with your family. There's a room booked in my name at the Private Island Spa for your use. I'll give you a call if I need to head back to New York ahead of schedule."

"We'd love to stay here, thank you, sir. Do you want us on standby?" Tuck asked.

Brant often needed last-minute flights, but this time he shook his head. "Nope. I'll give you at least a day advance notice if I want the plane. You two relax and forget about me and work for a while."

"Merry Christmas, sir," Tuck said with another solemn salute, but Michelle gave Brant a hug. It took him by surprise, but after an awkward moment, he hugged her back.

Michelle opened the cabin door, and Brant grabbed his jacket before descending the short mobile staircase the ground crew had rolled up to the aircraft.

"Uncle Brant! Uncle Brant!!"

He looked in the direction of the shouts to see a boy and girl jumping up and down and waving. He waved back and headed in their direction, but they ran up and threw themselves at him before he had a chance to brace for the onslaught.

He glanced around again before he spotted his sister Ellie.

"I may be seeing things, but you look a lot like my little brother." She joined in the group hug.

"Ellie!" Brant threw his arms around her. "It's really me. And I'm not so little!"

She hugged back tightly as the kids still held on.

"Who are these other people? What have you done with my munchkins?" Brant let go and stepped back to stare at the kids.

"I'm not a munchkin. I'm almost ten," the girl announced. She wore head-to-toe green, from a Kelly green headband threaded through her wavy, sandy-colored hair to neon-green sneakers, and everything in between.

"Ten?" Were they really so old? It had been longer than Brant had thought since he'd seen them, and they'd grown so much.

"I'm almost ten, too," the boy added and Brant ruffled his short, neat hair, causing the boy to instinctively smooth it over again with a shy nod.

"You're almost ten *minus* ten minutes! Don't forget that, Jenner." The girl stuck out her tongue for emphasis.

"Shut up, Sunday!" Jenner grimaced at his sister, then reached for Brant's hand again and held on, as if pulling him away from Sunday's evil influence, keeping Brant for himself.

"That sure sounds familiar," Ellie said with a laugh. "But with you it was only eight minutes. And you haven't caught up yet."

"I'll never stop trying." Brant grinned. When they were kids Ellie had lorded her eight-minute head start over him almost constantly.

"I know." She let out a sigh. "Sometimes I think it's all my fault you're so competitive."

"What, me, competitive?" He laughed. It felt good. It all felt good. The hugs from Ellie and the kids, the balmy breeze, the sun on his face. The salty tang of the air. The calm.

They climbed into the airport jeep, already loaded with Brant's luggage, then drove toward the Customs building. After dealing with paperwork, they were driven to the nearby pier where they would catch the launch to Taha'a.

"Did you bring it?" Sunday pulled at the hem of his shirt.

Jenner chimed in with a harder tug. "You did get it, right?" Both children's eyes were wide, hopeful, yet almost not-believing.

Brant glanced over at Ellie, eyebrows raised. "Get what?"

The kids erupted in shrieks. "You forgot? Ohmigod, nooooo!" Sunday wailed.

Ellie shook her head with a disapproving, down-turned mouth.

"What was I supposed to bring?" Brant wouldn't relent just yet.

"The tree!" Even Ellie joined in this time.

"Oh, right. You guys wanted a tree. Maple, right? For pancake syrup?"

Sunday's fists pounded into Brant's back. "Nooooooooooooooo."

"Good. 'Cause I didn't get a maple tree."

Just then one of the harbor staff drove up in a cart carrying a tall wooden crate, with a series of holes drilled in the sides.

Jenner ran his hands along the side of the crate. On tiptoes he could just reach the lowest hole and he peered in. Sunday ran up and pushed Jenner out of the way, poking her nose through the hole and inhaled. A joyous shout echoed off the tarmac. "Smells like Christmas tree!"

The kids jumped up and down, ran back, and threw themselves at Brant again. As he patted their heads he felt like a hero. He heard Ellie's relieved sigh as she hooked her arm around his. "Thanks for not forgetting." She turned to him and planted a kiss on his cheek.

"Don't I always keep my promises to the kids?"

Ellie's smile faded slightly. "I noticed how you qualified that statement."

A pang of guilt stabbed at Brant. "I know what you're going to say...."

"How many times over the past four years have you promised to visit? More than I care to count. I'm just so glad you made it this year. The kids would have been heartbroken if you'd canceled." She left "again" unspoken, but it settled there between them like a beached whale.

"But I'm here."

"And you're alone. What happened to AK? Or did you just make him up?" Ellie's gaze bored into Brant's.

"Well, that's a bit complicated. Things didn't quite work out as expected on that front."

Ellie's gaze softened and she tightened her grip on Brant's arm, drawing him in close. "I'm sorry about that. I was hoping maybe he was … special?"

Brant looked out toward the horizon, the bright sunlight glinting off the water. He took a breath, inhaling that amazing vanilla-tinged aroma that made this place unlike anywhere else on earth. "Not special enough."

"Is there anyone out there who could meet your high standards?"

"Probably not."

They both laughed and the kids ran over from the side of the boat to see what they were missing.

"Just promise me one thing, and one thing only."

"Sure, Sis, anything you want."

"While you're here, absolutely. No. Business. Period."

"Promise."

"If I catch you even sneaking a text, that's it. You're out. I'll dump you at the harbor and leave you there."

"Promise," Brant assured her. And he meant it, too. It felt great to be here, with Ellie and the kids, even if his big sister still intended to boss him around.

CHAPTER SIX

Thursday, December 23
French Polynesia

Alec orchestrated an elaborate game of phone tag with Big Ben all afternoon on Tuesday so he wouldn't have to admit he hadn't gotten Brant Linton's signature. Thankfully, Gina helped keep Whitman from connecting with Alec, and once he'd safely boarded his flight, she would give her boss the message that Alec was meeting with Linton the following day to finalize the deal. She wouldn't mention the tiny detail that any further communication between them would be taking place in French Polynesia.

Or so Alec hoped. He pored over the pitch book and contracts during the long flights, punctuated only by a stopover in LA. He needed to know the details inside and out so Linton couldn't find another reason to weasel out after Alec had gone above and beyond to put this deal together to Linton's exacting specifications.

With excitement and desperation balancing his exhaustion, Alec arrived in Bora Bora. Had he come on any other errand he would have enjoyed the gorgeous views as the plane came in low over stunning beaches like fine sugar and cerulean seas. If he succeeded with Linton, maybe he'd treat himself to one day of relaxation before heading back to New York.

Once he landed and cleared customs, Alec discovered he still had an uphill climb even before attempting to approach Brant Linton. He tried to arrange accommodation on Taha'a from the airport, thinking it might be easier once on the ground, only to discover there were no vacancies.

While Alec's fluent French eased communication, it did nothing to change his luck. No vacancies on Raiatea or Bora Bora, at any price level. He cabbed it to the harbor where he could take a ferry or hire a private water taxi to Taha'a.

He sat in the harbor waiting area, which smelled of fuel and salt and perhaps a little bit of fish. He'd exchanged his casual winter clothes for chinos and a short-sleeved cotton shirt from his favorite designer, and felt like a snake shedding its skin. The lazy breeze served merely to blow the humidity around, but the thatched roof kept the sun's heat from beating down too harshly. He looked at his watch again and sighed. It was a three-hour journey to Taha'a but there wasn't a ferry or water taxi in sight.

He'd been trying unsuccessfully to call Brant's cell phone since Tuesday morning in New York. He made sure to use *67 so Linton wouldn't see a series of missed calls from him, but the inability to make contact worried Alec. What if he arrived on Taha'a only to find out Linton *wasn't* there with his sister? Given the difficulty getting here, how much more problematic would it be to find out wherever Linton actually intended to spend Christmas?

There was nothing he could do for the moment, so Alec closed his eyes and took a deep calming breath, reminding himself to appreciate the beauty of his surroundings. Most Westerners considered these islands paradise, but instead of enjoying himself, he was rushing around trying to catch up to a guy who probably didn't want to be found. For the first time, Alec questioned his decision to come here.

The woman behind the harbor desk informed him that the water taxis were all out with passengers, so the ferry was his best option unless his hotel would be sending a private launch.

"I'm not staying at a hotel. Could you possibly suggest one?"

"You going to Taha'a without a hotel?"

"Yes, I've got to meet someone for work, but I couldn't get a reservation."

"Someone very important and very rich, I suppose?" She spoke with a low, throaty voice, and had a beautiful smile and an easy, natural laugh. Alec liked her accent, so different from the other French speakers he'd met around the world.

"You know Eleanor Linton?" he asked.

Her smile brightened. "Doctor Ellie? *Mais oui.* Everyone knows her. She is chief at the hospital on Raiatea."

"Yes, that's her."

"You are here to meet with Doctor Ellie?"

"No, her brother."

She nodded with evident pleasure. "Oh yes, Mr. Brant. He's very rich and important back in New York, I hear."

Alec nodded. "That's him, world famous."

"My cousin is living on Raiatea. He fixes boats at the marina for the very rich people who sail around the world. You should ask for him when you arrive. He will gladly help you find a place to stay. Ask for Tevala and tell him Miria sent you."

"Really?" Alec was skeptical. Why on earth would either of them want to help a total stranger? He asked her.

"Doctor Ellie has been very good to many people in these islands, saved many lives, especially children. If you are her friend or brother's friend, then we are happy to help."

"Thank you. I'll ask for him when I arrive."

While they had been chatting, several other passengers, mostly locals based on their clothing and lack of luggage, began arriving and the waiting room filled up. The ferry arrived twenty minutes late, practically considered early, given the relaxed attitude toward punctuality in the islands. With nearly everyone on vacation, who really needed to be on time? Even the locals had little desire to rush, a product of the climate.

Alec still thought in New York time and his blood pressure rose again as the debarking passengers shuffled off, and his fellow passengers shuffled just as slowly onboard. He fought the urge to push a couple of people out of the way and rush ahead of them. The ferry would still have to wait for everyone before departing, so he wouldn't save any time. But he would feel marginally less helpless here out of his element.

He paced around the deck of the ferry as it traveled between islands ringed with turquoise reefs, but he found himself unwinding as he watched the emerald peaks of Bora Bora fade in the distance. Maybe it was simply the stress of his situation and the long flight, or the humidity wearing him down, but by the time he finally arrived at Taha'a, he'd soaked up enough sun and sea salt and gorgeous scenery that he finally understood what enticed people to these islands for centuries.

As the ferry neared Taha'a, the larger island of Raiatea loomed behind, its chocolate mountains covered with green velvet, lending a beautiful but mysterious and imposing backdrop to the smaller and shorter island of Taha'a. In fact, the two islands were so close you could all but swim between them.

As they approached Taha'a Alec detected a marked difference in the air. A deep, sweet and familiar scent permeated his senses. *Vanilla?* What on earth? He sniffed the air a few times to be sure.

"*Oui*, it's vanilla," another passenger, an elderly Frenchman, confirmed. "Taha'a is famous for vanilla. You can smell it all year round, especially during autumn, when they lay the pods in the sun to dry before shipping them far away."

Who knew? This trip got more and more interesting with each passing hour. The farther Alec got from civilization, the more there was to see and discover. At first he'd wondered why anyone ever left Manhattan, a city he loved for its fast pace and constant surprises.

Now he wondered why he'd stayed cooped up in offices and boardrooms, and why Brant Linton ever left these islands to head back to the States.

* * * *

Brant's usual high energy didn't last long on his first day in the islands. They'd barely slowed down long enough for lunch at the house, before the kids insisted on treating him a ride around the island in the family launch. He couldn't deny that the fresh vanilla-tinged sea breezes and the sun's warmth didn't make him feel alive again, but after only a couple of hours in the heat and humidity, he was exhausted and had to refuse repeated requests to stop at one beach or another. He begged off further adventures until he caught up with the time and climate change, and they all headed home.

Henri, Ellie's husband, worked as a chef at one of Taha'a's five-plus-star resorts, but took the evening off to prepare a special welcome dinner, which Brant ruined by falling asleep between the fresh crab, prepared with ribbons of local fruit and vegetables, and whatever delight came next.

The following morning, Brant's internal batteries were fully recharged by the time the kids—Sunday in another all-green affair and Jenner in every color *but* green—burst into his room to wake him up. He slipped into a scratchy new pair of swim trunks while they bounded downstairs to wait for him in the kitchen. As usual, he'd slept nude, and it wasn't until morning he'd discovered his suitcase contained little more than the bare necessities.

Apparently AK, in a fit of pique, had removed everything from Brant's suitcase except for a toothbrush, a bottle of designer sunscreen, the swim trunks, a stretched-out old T-shirt Brant wore to work out, and a pair of tennis shoes. At least his other suitcase, filled with gifts for the kids, hadn't been sabotaged.

Brant shrugged off the mean-spirited gesture as further proof he was better off without AK, and headed downstairs for breakfast of fresh local fruit and pancakes. While the adults sipped strong black coffee, Ellie got called into the hospital on Raiatea to deliver twins who were several weeks premature.

Well rested and up to any challenge, Brant agreed to the kid's suggestion of a circle tour of the island by bicycle. They spent most of the day on the winding roads around the island. The kids showed Brant their favorite spots and reacquainted him with the places he recalled fondly from previous visits. The island was livelier than he remembered and he spotted a few new small guest houses, but overall it retained its low-key charm.

Even the light exertion reminded him how little time he spent out of the office. Soon his creaky joints and stiff muscles sang with the endorphin rush. He only thought about work once or twice.

His body came alive after prolonged neglect, and craved additional stimulation. A flicker of arousal surprised Brant as he imagined not AK but with a pang of guilt at the realization he'd left the attractive Alec Compton hanging back in New York after dumping so many new contract demands on him.

Mid-afternoon they were relaxing and cooling off with fruity drinks at a nameless local favorite café, when Brant's phone vibrated in his pocket. Ellie's name flashed on the screen, so he answered immediately.

"Brant, I've got a huge surprise for you!" She practically quivered over the phone. He couldn't remember the last time she'd been this excited except the time she'd played a very unpleasant practical joke on him during anatomy when they'd been in med school together.

"What is it?"

"Not what, who!"

"Who, what?"

"No. Who," she said again.

"Okay, am I Abbott or Costello in this conversation?" Brant let out a laugh that had the kids bouncing at his side, their eyes wide with questions.

"Your surprise is who I was just talking to." Now she was nearly whispering and Brant found himself clutching the phone more tightly to his ear. "Maybe he's more special than you originally thought."

"Who?" Brant repeated until Ellie's words sunk in. She'd been repeating his words from the previous day. About AK.

AK was here?

Brant had already pushed AK onto the lawyer's plate, thus putting him out of mind, and the idea of seeing him again so soon wasn't at all appealing, especially after that bullshit with the suitcase.

"He's *here*? I didn't dream he'd actually show up on his own." Apparently AK wasn't ready to give up the chance to snorkel with the rich and famous. Something about that typical opportunism really pissed Brant off. He'd resigned himself to cutting things off with AK and found he was happier than he'd expected being able to spend time with the family on his own. Now AK had to show up fuck up Brant's new plans?

"Are you still there, Brant?"

"You know, I don't want to see him after all. He left me, and not in a particularly nice way. I'm not looking to sort it out just yet."

Fucking stalker was the thought really going through his brain.

"You can't just blow him off that easily. He flew all the way out here so you should at least listen to what he has to say."

"No, Ellie. Please don't even invite him over, or anything, okay?"

"Just come home soon, Brant."

Her reply took too long and Brant's stomach lurched.

Fuck. AK could already be at Ellie's house. Brant admitted being a tiny bit impressed he could figure out how to get here all by himself. Apparently Brant's lawyer hadn't canceled the credit cards in time to stop AK buying a plane ticket. He'd have to deal with it in person. But Brant already knew this was going to fuck up the rest of his long-overdue holiday visit here.

He paid for the drinks, and the three of them got back on the bikes and pedaled in the direction of home. Brant couldn't join in the kids' frivolity, no matter how hard he tried. His good mood was shattered, and it was going to get a lot worse before it got better, that much was certain.

Despite making a game out of pedaling as slowly as possible without falling over, eventually they arrived at Ellie and Henri's. Leaving the bikes on the grass in front of the house, the kids ran in through the front door, and Brant followed with a heavy heart. He could hear Ellie's voice from the kitchen, talking to someone he couldn't yet see.

Sunday and Jenner beat Brant into the kitchen, and now his "reunion" with AK would be even more embarrassing and awkward. He seriously considered walking right back out the door and riding Henri's bike to the farthest beach where he'd camp out until the coast was clear. If only he hadn't given his reservation to Tuck and Michelle!

He steeled himself and entered the kitchen.

CHAPTER SEVEN

Brant dreaded seeing AK again, and expected the worst. Instead of finding Ellie sipping spicy peach tea with AK, it was Alec Compton who sat in her bright kitchen wearing rumpled Chinos and an impeccably cut sport shirt that looked like it had been tailor made for his surprisingly well-toned upper body.

Brant wasn't sure how to process this startling turn of events. How had he forgotten how attracted he'd been to Compton only a few days earlier in his office? The undeniable spark between them had put him off his game and complicated the deal Compton offered.

Now, here, half a world away, and despite the un-businesslike thoughts he'd harbored about Alec, Brant still wasn't thrilled with this uninvited guest in Ellie's home. While he'd initially been flattered that Alec had followed him, it was only to get his signature on the Turner Foods buyout. The realization that Alec's perseverance was strictly business and not personal somehow stung even worse than AK's treachery.

Even so, Brant was more interested than ever in signing onto Alec's deal.

Their gazes locked for only a fraction of a second, too briefly for Brant to read Alec's mood, or to formulate his own response.

"You look like you've seen a ghost!" Ellie said.

The kids ran up to Alec, eager to meet the stranger. They stood near the table, expressions hopeful, but somehow knowing better than to jump all over him.

"Alec, this is Jenner." Ellie began the introductions.

Alec stood and turned toward Jenner.

"Jen-nerd!" Sunday corrected and Brant couldn't help cracking up. He noticed Alec responded only with a smile.

And *I'm* Sunday." She held out a hand as regally as a queen might. Brant wasn't sure if she expected Alec to shake it or kiss it.

"Nice to meet you both." Alec held out his own hand and shook hands first with Sunday, and then with Jenner, who looked confused, then very pleased. Few adults shook hands with ten-year-olds, but Jenner seemed to take it as a supreme compliment.

"Sunday, is it? I'd have to say, you really look more like a Friday to me."

Sunday, usually hard to impress, was now putty in Alec's hands. She gushed and giggled in a way Brant hadn't seen before. "I'm named for Uncle Brant, you know."

Alec glanced over, and Brant's mood deteriorated further. So much for keeping any secrets or mystery.

"So that's what the 'S' is for? S. Brant Linton." Alec gave a satisfied smile, and Brant *almost* wanted to smack it off and considered retaliation for showing up here in the middle of his up-to-now enjoyable family holiday.

"Brant, is that the best greeting you've got for Alec after such a long trip?" Ellie's tone made Brant feel even more like a misbehaving child.

After his shock—and some small relief— at not having to confront AK, Brant took a moment to process Alec's presence. How the fucking hell had he found Brant at Ellie's house? Of course on such a small island, everyone knows everything about everyone else, and all he'd need to do was to ask around. Easy research for someone like Alec Compton.

"I don't care what happened in New York, Brant. Alec's staying for dinner." Ellie's announcement left no room for disobedience.

Alec grinned and Brant definitely wanted to smack him. Or get him to take that shirt off.

"Why don't you two have some privacy, over in the den, maybe?" Ellie motioned down the hallway.

Alec grinned and a corner of his mouth turned up playfully. "Privacy. Yes."

Brant's blood pressure hit a new high. He gripped Alec's elbow, trying to ignore the residual fireworks at touching him again—and steered him toward the den and shut the door. He'd give the presumptuous Alec Compton a piece of his mind! What was he thinking coming here and invading Brant's personal life?

Alec flashed a delightfully cheeky grin. "Care to explain why your sister thinks we're *dating?*"

That gorgeous smile caught Brant off guard and every insult on the tip of his tongue vanished. Instead, he stood, taking in the sight of Alec in his well-fitted pants and body-hugging shirt. Heat crept up Brant's spine as he fought for something to say. He wasn't sure what flustered him more: Alec being suddenly privy to Brant's personal life, or Brant's internal recognition that dating Alec would have been pleasant under any circumstances other than these.

"I take it I'm not your type, Alec?" Brant had no idea what prompted him to say *that*. Why on earth was he upset that Alec seemed offended by the idea they were dating?

"Thing is, you absolutely are my type, Brant. But you probably didn't realize I might be yours." Alec's chuckle was light, genuine and as disturbingly sexy as the rest of him.

Brant attempted to shake off that bombshell with a sideways nod. "Well, that aside, you have no right to be here."

"Well, you're here, so I'm here."

A quick double-tap sounded at the door before it opened and Ellie entered, a huge smile on her face, and carrying a tray with fruit-garnished glasses of what could have been iced tea or Long Island Iced Tea.

"I've got the perfect idea, Brant. Since Alec couldn't get a reservation at any of the hotels, so I think he should stay here, with us, as *originally* planned." She speared Brant with her gaze.

Brant blinked a couple of times, hoping he'd misheard her. Alec's expectant expression had progressed to an annoyingly satisfied smirk.

"No, Ellie, I'm not sure that's a good idea." He flashed a warning to Alec.

"After he came all this way and he just said 'where you are, I am' or something to that effect?"

So she'd been eavesdropping. Typical Ellie.

"Look, Ellie, this is just not your business. I appreciate your ... zeal, but—"

She cut him off. "You just don't know what's good for you. Never have." She took Brant by the arm and turned him away from Alec and continued in a low voice. "All you ever think about is work. If you don't just step back and relax, you're never going to find the right person or settle down. Take the time to work through things with Alec, not just run away like you always do."

Brant glanced over his shoulder to see Alec watching them. *Fucking hell.* If this wasn't the most embarrassing thing ever to happen to him. How could he present a businesslike demeanor with Alec knowing these personal details, from his real first name to his busybody sister, to the fact he'd just broken up with the real boyfriend?

But he knew Ellie well enough to accept she wouldn't stop meddling as long as she wanted to play matchmaker. What irony. Here she was pushing him into a business deal during what was a supposedly no-business-allowed family holiday?

Brant had the choice of defusing the Alec bomb by fessing up to his original charade or by just giving in to Ellie. She'd kill Brant one way or another as soon as she discovered the truth. And Alec still looked far too cheerful at Brant's discomfiture.

In the face of unwinnable odds, Brant took the path of least resistance.

"Sure, Alec. Why don't you stay here, with us?"

"Good. That's settled." Now Ellie looked smug. "Now, to make sure you two lovebirds concentrate on each other for a while, let me have your phone, Brant." She held out a hand. "Alec, I don't expect *you* get called every ten minutes needing to prevent a financial meltdown that would destroy the universe now, do you?"

"Uh, hardly ever."

Reluctantly, Brant pulled his cell out of his pocket and handed it to her. He really didn't need it after all. Aside from the dozen or so missed calls from a blocked number he'd gotten over the past day, no one had tried to contact him here. Everything else would simply have to wait until he could steal his phone back from Ellie. He and Alec could handle their business face-to-face, using Alec's phone if necessary.

Had he only been lying to himself about his intention to relax during this trip, without being connected to every tiny swing of the market? He'd give it a try as long as he could. Who knew, maybe it wouldn't be as excruciatingly painful as it sounded.

Yeah, it would. Brant already felt withdrawal symptoms and his fingers itched for the phone.

Conveniently, Alec had brought his bags with him to Ellie's. Fucker had probably arranged all of this while Brant was still out cycling with the twins. Ellie batted her eyes at Alec, then glared at Brant until he got Alec's luggage and carried it upstairs. Alec stood back and let Ellie take control, but Brant could tell he was enjoying this far too much, considering he needed Brant's signature on that contract.

"Didn't know you had two guest rooms," Brant called down over his shoulder as he climbed the stairs.

"We don't. Just the one that you're in."

Brant stopped two steps from the top. Ohhh, no. Ellie wasn't going to push Alec on him like that. The guest room wasn't really spacious enough for two people. It might be fine for a couple, but despite his fleeting daydreams, he and Alec were absolutely *not* a couple.

CHAPTER EIGHT

"Do you want to see what I brought you?" They were upstairs, alone, and Alec dared another flirty look at Brant. He knew he'd already pushed Brant farther than was prudent, considering Alec was here out of desperation.

It had certainly be worth it to see how his arrival had ruffled the feathers of the eminently self-possessed Brant Linton.

"Only if you're talking about the deal." Brant shifted back to a more authoritative tone out of his sister's hearing, probably so Alec wouldn't get any ideas.

"What else would I be talking about?" Alec cocked one eyebrow and went over to his bag, rifled through it, and brought out two identical thick blue binders. He handed one to Brant.

"I certainly hope you're not going to charge Linton Holdings a courier fee on this." Brant avoided Alec's gaze. "You really must need this deal in the worst way to not only follow me, but mislead my sister like that. There will be hell to pay when she finds out."

"She wants you to get back with your boyfriend, and based on how long it took you to walk in the front door, you weren't exactly looking forward to seeing him again. I almost thought you were glad to see *me*. I take things didn't end well?" Alec admitted he was more curious than he had any right to be.

"None of your fucking business." As soon as the words were out of his mouth, a little tremor played across Brant's lips. "I'd rather not get into my personal life any more than absolutely necessary."

"But Ellie wants you to patch things up at least as much as she wants to make sure you don't try to do any business while you're here."

"Are you blackmailing me? Threatening to tell Ellie if I don't do your deal?" Brant peered at Alec with sharp eyes, back firmly in control. "I'm willing to incur Ellie's wrath if necessary. I don't need to do this deal."

Alec paused to appraise Linton. He'd gotten hot under the collar and the room felt uncomfortably warm now, but it put a light in Brant's eyes that drew Alec in like a magnet. He forced himself to take a step back and cool down a bit because being this close to Brant made it difficult to think clearly.

"I know you don't. But it's a good deal with very little risk to you. I know you wouldn't have made me jump through all those hoops if you hadn't been interested. You're too busy to have given me more than ten seconds of your time."

Brant blinked and waited, but something in his gaze told Alec he'd guessed right. And that this negotiation wasn't just business. "Maybe I can help you and you can help me. Ben Whitman is so far up my ass over this deal, I can taste his shampoo, and honestly, I need more from you than you need from me. But if it will help you avoid disappointing your sister, I'll continue the charade as your boyfriend, and you'll—"

"Thank you by signing the papers?"

"Just look at the contract I've put together. That's all I ask. If you decide you really don't want the deal, then I'll face Whitman's consequences. But no matter what, I won't let on why I'm really here to your sister."

Alec tried to sound more laid-back than he felt.

"Then what's the big rush, Compton?"

Alec took a deep breath. "I have to close it by year-end."

Another gleam flashed in Brant's eyes.

Alec hoped he hadn't just signed his own death warrant by owning up that he was on a strict deadline. Then again, from everything he'd read on game theory, he'd offered up some information and if Brant wanted to keep playing he'd get more by not using it against Alec.

"I'm sure we can come to some agreement, especially after you went to such lengths to track me down."

"You told your assistant if it was a life-or-death situation, and it could just be my death."

"So, you show me your contract—"

"And I'll show you what a good boyfriend I can be." Alec moved a step closer and flashed a teasing grin at Brant.

The heat in the gaze Brant returned nearly ignited the entire room.

This could be fun, or Alec could be playing with fire. Well, if he was going to get burned, he couldn't think of a better way to go.

* * * *

Brant had to step back two paces. Being this close to Alec was detrimental to his equilibrium. Damn him for letting Brant know he was gay and how much he would enjoy their little masquerade.

Thankfully, scents and sounds emanating from downstairs told him that Henri was home. Time for a safer topic of conversation.

"Did I mention my brother-in-law is a French chef?"

"I'll make do with the hardship." Alec flashed another brilliant smile and Brant found his amusement infectious.

Henri was in the kitchen assembling a platter containing a whole grilled fish while Ellie ferried another platter with bright-orange lobsters to the large, rather rustic table on the veranda off the dining room.

"Can I help with anything? Alec asked first in English and again in French. Henri responded, clearly assigning Alec a task, and Brant stiffened. He hoped Alec wasn't going to be a toady the whole time, making everyone like him, then blame Brant for being an asshole when they never saw Alec again.

Introducing a "partner" to the family was always fraught with pitfalls, even when he was just a fake boyfriend.

Brant reminded himself of the pros here: better terms on a deal that was already good, and someone to keep Ellie from nagging or trying to set him up the rest of the trip.

Despite the escalating heat level, Alec was manipulating him. Brant questioned just how far Alec would go for a deal. And how far Alec could be trusted.

On the other hand, if Brant was forced to endure a fake boyfriend for a few days, he really couldn't imagine a more delicious prospect. He and Alec could sneak off without explanation, and Ellie would never know they were doing business, and not getting busy.

He sipped the glass of sparkling wine Ellie handed him and smiled as he watched Alec help Henri arrange platters on the dinner table.

"So tell us all about yourself, Alec," Ellie started in as soon as decently possible during dinner, ever the master of subtlety, Brant thought. He cringed and glanced at Alec who didn't appear fazed by all the attention he'd generated with Brant's family.

"Where are you from?"

"What's it like to be on Broadway?"

"How'd you meet Brant?"

The questions flew and Alec grinned and settled back in his chair. He threw Brant a coy, slightly nervous smile.

"My father was in international finance. Ex-pat for a huge American bank, at the time considered one of the most prestigious in the world. But when my dad worked for them he had one of the best jobs on Wall Street."

At the words "Wall Street" Ellie's face sort of scrunched up in a particularly unsatisfied way and she glared at Brant. It was only fifty percent strength, but it still packed plenty of heat, and he tried to flash a warning to Alec, but Alec wasn't paying attention.

"So my parents were living in Switzerland when I was born. They speak *Schweizerdeutsch* there, a local variant of German nobody else speaks, but we also had to learn French in school.

"That's why you speak French?" Ellie asked.

"Ah, that explains the accent," Henri added. I couldn't place it, but now you say it, I recognize it! Not exactly Swiss accent. Between Swiss and Yankee." He smiled and nodded with satisfaction.

"What was Switzerland like?" Sunday asked.

"Cold. You'd hate it." Everyone laughed. "But so beautiful I never noticed. I grew up with the languages, but my mom had so much trouble sometimes she'd look like she wanted to cry when we went shopping. I'll never forget one day at dinner. My mom and I had been to a small bakery that day and she was telling my dad she thought she'd broken through her language barrier. 'I went in with my list,' she said, 'and I told the clerk what I needed and we had such a nice chat. I got everything, and she even gave us some of a special cake she doesn't put on display, just saves for her best customers.'

"My dad was very excited, since he'd been worried at her usual frustration with communicating, until I explained, 'Mom, you were speaking *Schweizerdeutsch*, but the lady in the bakery was talking English back to you.'"

Everyone broke into laughter, even the kids.

Brant had skimmed over a report on Alec's background before their first meeting, and he knew about Alec's education and previous work experience. But hearing him tell such a personal anecdote brought him alive, far beyond the mere sum of the information on the page. Brant found himself caught up in his charm, then remembered he should already know these things about his "boyfriend" and risked Ellie sensing their ruse.

"Tell us about when you and Brant first met." Ellie gave an indulgent grin. She was as caught up as anyone, but Brant still wondered if at some level she was testing out their relationship.

"Of course I already knew who he was. Everyone in New York does." Alec threw Brant a charming lovey-dovey look before turning back to Ellie. "I had wanted to meet him, but the first time he spoke to me, I could barely speak. He completely overwhelmed me. I couldn't believe he was even more attractive and more fascinating in real life than I'd imagined. And I couldn't wait to see him again." Alec's gaze shifted to something on the table and Brant thought he might have seen the tiniest hint of color on Alec's cheeks and the tips of his ears. He'd played the part perfectly, without obvious lies or inventing something too fantastic to be believed. Hell, from the way Alec gazed at him, Brant believed they were in love.

"I think it's just about bedtime, *mes chatons*," Henri said to a chorus of disappointment from the twins. "Alec must be very tired from his journey. You will have plenty of time to grill him during the rest of the trip."

The kids were sent off to bed, and Ellie gave Brant a look implying he ought to hurry up and get Alec alone. Brant recalled his own exhausted first evening and knew despite Alec's seemingly bottomless energy, the time difference and jet lag would soon catch up hard.

"Right, we're heading upstairs, too." Brant felt torn between the idea of spending the night with Alec, which he'd thought about all during dinner, and worrying he might seem too eager to his pretend boyfriend. But Alec had played up the coy banter earlier, so Brant played along. "Before Alec's too tired …."

Alec had the good sense to look slightly embarrassed, but he slipped his hand into Brant's, tangling their fingers, which shot sparks through Brant's body. He certainly didn't need that.

Upstairs, it only got worse. Their bathroom was small, so Alec undressed in the middle of the room. Brant pulled off his own shirt and tossed it on the dresser and glanced over to see Alec folding up his shirt and shorts. He was still wearing his boxer-briefs.

Brant enjoyed the view in his peripheral vision and decided that his usual habit of sleeping nude might not be such a good idea, unless he wanted their pretend relationship to turn a lot more genuine.

Alec washed up and brushed his teeth thoroughly as Brant folded his own clothes. By the time Brant finished in the bathroom, Alec was under the covers in bed, propped up on one elbow, watching and waiting.

They hadn't spoken since they had come upstairs and Brant felt uncomfortable. What was Alec expecting? How far did he want to go? There was only one bed and he'd already gotten in. Brant glanced toward the armchair in one corner.

"There's room for both of us in here." Alec's cocky grin indicated he was enjoying Brant's discomfiture. Alec held up the sheet, giving Brant an inviting look at his body. All of his body: Alec had slipped out of his shorts and was nude. Brant blinked, debating, hoping his own cock wouldn't react to the sight of Alec's.

"The chair ...." Brant half-mumbled.

"Do you really want to spend the night in the chair? Alone?" Alec's gaze bore into Brant.

"No."

Alec ruffled the sheet again. "Problem solved. Don't worry. I can keep my hands to myself. If that's what you want."

That wasn't what Brant wanted, not at all. He wanted Alec's hands all over him, but it wouldn't do to actually say that. Would it? On the other hand, as long as Alec was willing, who would it hurt?

Brant slid between the sheets, and Alec settled back onto his side of the bed, his thigh brushing up against Brant's, sending the already familiar electricity straight to Brant's cock and burning deep into his core. Had it been accidental or was Alec waiting for Brant to make a definite move? Brant turned away as he reached toward the lamp on the bedside table and clicked it off.

When he turned back, Alec's head was on the pillow and his eyes were closed. In the now-silent house, Brant heard slow, deep, even breaths.

Alec was already asleep.

Problem solved. Brant found himself slightly offended Alec had drifted off to sleep so easily, but at least it postponed having to make a decision one way or another about how to handle being in bed with him.

Should Brant even consider some casual fun? That's how things had started out with AK. But Alec wasn't AK. And this wasn't a relationship. *Alec* wasn't here for fun; he'd only come here for a signature to save his job. For all Alec's charm and playfulness, he'd followed Brant to Taha'a for work, not for pleasure.

Alec's beautiful face, his gorgeous, desirable body, and the undeniable spark between them meant Brant would have to be even more diligent than usual about analyzing this deal.

At least that's what he reminded himself as he too began to fall under the spell Alec had already cast on the rest of the family.

CHAPTER NINE

Friday, December 24
Taha'a

After preparing far too much food for breakfast, Henri departed for the resort. Ellie had already left for the hospital on Raiatea. She wanted to ensure that all of her patients were well attended before she took a rare full day off for Christmas.

She had written another list of suggestions for the day's activities, and Henri had prepared a sumptuous lunch basket from the previous night's leftovers. It would make a wonderful picnic lunch wherever Alec, Brant and the kids decided to go.

At the urging of Sunday and Jenner, the four of them went sailing on *Premiere Cru* in order to give Alec the best tour of the island. The plan included a visit to the lovely beach on the other side of the island for leisurely day of sunning and swimming. Alec stuffed Brant's SPF60 designer sunscreen in the bag of supplies and they headed to the dock jutting out behind the house.

The constant presence of the twins kept Brant and Alec on their best behavior on all fronts. Even though Brant itched to discuss the Turner Foods deal, it would simply have to wait until later. Along with his physical longing for Alec. Instead, the day served as a fun way to get to know each other in ways probably neither of them anticipated.

As he was the day before, Alec was good company and handled Sunday and Jenner perfectly. Though he hadn't sailed much, he caught on quickly and the crew of four easily maneuvered the luxurious yacht through the calm, clear water.

Jenner won the coin toss to captain on the trip out, and Sunday would be captain on the return trip. Alec good-naturedly followed directions with assistance from Brant.

"So, Brant is this your boat?" Alec asked as they rounded one tip of the island. The breeze tousled his honey-colored hair and Brant had trouble paying attention to anything else.

"It was, but I gave it to Henri and Ellie when they moved here. They get far more use out of it than I ever could."

"I suppose it's a good incentive to visit them?" Alec trimmed and tied off the sail as instructed by Captain Jenner, muscles rippling under his skin. Already a few caramel-colored freckles dotted his shoulders.

"I wish I managed a trip more than every three or four years."

"Is that all? I'd never go home again if I didn't have to earn a living." The way Alec appreciated the island and the boat intensified Brant's guilt. "Sorry, that came out wrong. I can see you love your job."

"I do." But Alec's comments made Brant see his life from a different perspective, through Alec's eyes.

The beach they chose for lunch was even more enchanting than Brant remembered from his last trip. They anchored the boat just off shore and dove into the crystal clear water, chasing away bright-colored fish.

The powdered-sugar sand was blindingly white, so fine and smooth and felt heavenly between his toes. While the kids were occupied, Brant felt Alec's gaze on him more than once, heating up the day far more than the sun. They gave in to a mutual desire for touch under the guise of slathering sunscreen on each other.

Alec's hands promised more, later, when they were alone and Brant's fingers returned the message.

After lunch, Alec wandered down the road with the twins and returned with dripping ice cream cones heaped with pastel-colored tropical flavors. Watching Alec's tongue curl and lick was torture.

They swam and played and napped in between the kids asking a million and one questions. Alec gamely answered, deftly avoiding topics that might reveal the truth about his identity and their true relationship. Even so, Brant wondered more than once during the day how much was truth and how much simply a performance. Either way, spending time with Alec was sheer pleasure. He wrapped Brant around his finger as easily as Sunday and Jenner.

* * * *

Once home, the kids rushed through dinner and encouraged the adults to eat more quickly so they could get to the highlight of the day: decorating the tree.

"I get it now," Alec commented when Sunday encouraged everyone to eat much faster. "I thought it might be a local tradition to have an undecorated tree and no presents."

"We always do the tree on Christmas Eve, then Uncle Brant can put the presents under it," Jenner explained as he helped clear the table.

"Presents?" Brant joked. "All I did was bring the tree."

With Henri still at work, Brant and Alec insisted on doing dishes, and Ellie gathered the decorations for the tree. She had several boxes scattered in the family room and the kids were digging through impatiently when Alec and Brant joined them.

"I haven't seen these for ages! You still have those ones we made in fourth grade?" Brant looked like a kid again as he picked up one old ornament after another.

Alec stood back and watched for a few minutes. During their enjoyable day masquerading as lovers for the kids, Alec kept the boundaries of their relationship clearly in view, despite knowing how much he'd enjoy coloring outside the lines. But tonight, for the first time since he and Brant had come to their agreement, Alec felt out of place, an outsider observing a happy and close family.

He watched Brant's face light up as he dug through the box of family memories. While the twins haphazardly hung tinsel and ornaments, Brant and Ellie bantered, reliving old Christmases and their long-standing sibling rivalry.

Though Alec had seen Brant interacting with his family, brushing his teeth, and in his underwear, the man still retained an air of power and elegance about him. The commanding presence, part of his success in the business world, never quite dissolved for Alec. But now, retelling family stories, some embarrassing, some sweet, Brant at last became a normal-sized human and not an untouchable corporate superhero.

He was genuine and worth getting to know in a romantic way Alec hadn't even considered before. Certainly the interest in a physical relationship was mutual, but Alec let himself entertain the idea of even more.

The problem was he'd painted himself into a corner by coming here for a deal and not for personal or romantic reasons, and Alec knew Brant wouldn't likely forgive him for that, no matter what happened when they were alone.

CHAPTER TEN

By the time Henri got home, the adults were pleasantly tipsy from glasses of port and the tree was nearly finished. Ellie went upstairs to get the first batch of presents to place under it while the kids filled Henri in on their wonderful day sailing, sunning and snorkeling with Alec and Brant.

"Uncle Brant, you look like the lobster from last night's dinner!" Jenner remarked.

Brant had dutifully applied and reapplied sunscreen every few hours, with Alec's welcome assistance, but it wasn't until now he felt the tell-tale sting and itch. It was his own fault, and even the most expensive sunscreen in New York couldn't defeat the French Polynesian sun, even if the label did say "SPF 60."

"Mom'll know what to do," Sunday insisted, though she couldn't help giggle at his predicament. She pressed a finger to his skin, leaving a round white spot that quickly returned to its bright red hue. "Yup, you're done."

"Uncle Brant's a doctor, too, you know!" Jenner defended Brant's honor in a way that touched him.

"Doctor?" Alec asked.

"Went to med school, but decided not to practice. Kind of a long story." Thankfully Ellie came downstairs and changed the subject before Alec inquired about a subject Brant had no desire to discuss. He didn't want to be rude or evasive after such a pleasant day together.

"Oh my, Brant. What happened? You were fine until just now."

"I know. Sunburn usually doesn't present like this. Besides I had SPF 60 on all day. I was good. Alec helped." Brant threw an appropriate glance in his direction.

"This isn't sunburn," Ellie announced in her MD voice. "Let me see that bottle of sunscreen."

"I'll get it." Alec ran upstairs to retrieve it.

Ellie squinted at the ingredient list. "Yup, here we go. This has kiwi in it. Did you realize that?"

Brant took the bottle from her. "No. A–" He cut himself short, before mentioning AK had purchased it, when Alec was supposed to be AK. "Even so, I'm only slightly allergic, not enough to cause this reaction."

"You used it all day. Why did it just happen now?" Alec asked.

"Probably the compound in the kiwi was enhanced by something we had at dinner, magnifying the allergen's effect," Ellie explained. "Let me get something from my bag for you."

Brant's skin felt uncomfortable and hot. At least he wasn't in massive discomfort, or in danger of anaphylactic shock. AK had known about the allergy, but Brant didn't want to suspect AK had bought a product with kiwi on purpose.

Would he go this far to get back at Brant? Taking the furniture and unpacking Brant's clothing were one thing, but given Brant's allergy, exposure to kiwi could have had a much more serious effect. AK hadn't known it was a mild allergy, only that it kept Brant from eating kiwi.

"This cream should take care of pain and redness. Alec can make sure to get all those hard-to-reach spots." Ellie grinned mischievously as she handed the tube to Alec.

"I definitely will make sure not to miss anything." Alec chuckled and nearly knocked over what remained in his glass of port.

Brant wanted to punch both of them this time. How could they enjoy his suffering so much?

"I guess those pricey creams aren't really worth the money, are they?" Ellie said. "Nothing like the good old-fashioned stuff, even if it doesn't have the delicate aroma of some rare orchid grown only on one hilltop in Hawaii, or whatever crap lies they use to market that stuff."

"Mom, you said 'crap,'" Sunday announced with her usual officious tone, making everyone else laugh.

"You're right. How much is that?" Ellie asked. "We pay a fine here for cursing," she told Alec.

"Two euros."

"Damn, that's expensive!" Brant responded.

"Two for you, too," Sunday added and held out a hand.

Brant grinned and reached for his wallet to pay his debt to society.

"How much is a really bad word?" Alec asked.

"Fifty euros!" Sunday pocketed Brant's fine with a satisfied grin, then bounded into the kitchen where she apparently put the money into a jar of some sort, based on the clinking sounds.

"What do you do with the money?" Alec asked.

"At the end of the month we count it all out, and the kids decide. Usually they donate some to charity and put what's left in a savings account," Henri explained.

"Brant, try out that cream. It's got a mild analgesic, but if it's not strong enough, I can give you an injection."

"We should probably do this upstairs," Alec said with his irresistible grin.

Upstairs? We? Brant wondered what he'd be getting himself into.

Inside their room, Alec stared expectantly at Brant.

"I know you won't be able to reach all the spots. You need help, but I can get Ellie or Henri if you prefer …."

Brant didn't want Ellie or Henri right now. He wanted Alec, had been wanting him all day, but despite Alec's sexy banter, Brant didn't know how much was real and how much just an act. Brant had let himself enjoy Alec's company, but in front of the kids it had been safe.

Now, alone, Brant wasn't so sure how he'd handle his undeniable attraction to Alec. And given the pending deal, nothing physical between them was a particularly advisable.

"I'm sure this cream will be much more effective on your skin than on that robe."

"Right." Brant hesitated a moment before he let the robe slip down his shoulders. He was wearing boxers and he'd been in a swimsuit all day, but now he felt a surge of embarrassment as Alec looked him over appraisingly. He held out a hand to Alec. "Squeeze some ointment out. I'll do my chest and you can help with my back."

"Sure." Alec's voice held a note of disappointment.

Brant began to smooth cream onto his chest. Cool and soothing, it made his nipples peak. Or maybe it was the way Alec touched him. Alec's fingers were gentle, firm enough not to be ticklish, and already familiar enough with all of Brant's most sensitive spots that Brant felt his cock hardening, tenting out his shorts. An embarrassing damp spot appeared and he shifted his stance but it did no good. His cock bobbed slightly, the head dragging across the soft fabric, getting Brant even more aroused.

Alec took his time, smoothing over every exposed inch of Brant's back, neck, shoulders, along each shoulder blade, down his spine, across his waist and hips. Alec knelt behind Brant, starting at his ankles and smoothing up the calf, then thigh, with attention to the sensitive skin of the inner thigh.

"Would you like some more?" Alec asked, with a little catch to his voice.

"More?" Brant nearly moaned. He'd had been so focused on Alec's motions he'd barely spread any cream at all yet.

Alec stood up and moved in front of Brant, immediately spotting Brant's hard-on but not mentioning it.

"I can finish the front for you," he offered, the invitation plain in both his voice and expression.

"Yeah." The huskiness in Brant's voice made the word sound much more needy than he'd wanted, but Alec smiled and continued where Brant had left off mid-chest, and smoothed his way dangerously close to Brant's now-aching and obvious erection.

Alec moved his hands more slowly and deliberately. Was he trying to torture Brant or did he enjoy this as much as Brant did? With anyone else what might happen next would be easy and natural, but Brant still didn't know exactly what Alec was offering or expecting. How far would he go to get Brant to sign a contract? He'd already come half way around the world, so sleeping with Brant didn't seem out of the question.

But something in Brant couldn't just take so easily what Alec offered. He'd always kept sex and business separate before, no matter how attractive he'd found someone he'd been working with. Now Alec knelt in front of him, smoothing cream on his legs before he reached up. Alec's fingers grazed a nipple, and it hardened and ached the way his cock did. A tiny moan escaped his lips, and Alec responded with firmer pressure on the nipple and edged closer.

"All done," Alec announced and Brant's stomach did a flip. "But I can take care of that as well." Alec inclined his head, indicating Brant's cock, but making no attempt to stand up or move away.

Yes, yes, yes, yes, yes, pleeeeeeaaaaaase, Brant's body shouted.

Alec's fingers lingered at the waistband of Brant's shorts and he met Brant's gaze. If Alec didn't want this, want *Brant*, he was a better actor than AK, because Brant saw his own need and desire mirrored in Alec's eyes. Brant put his hands on Alec's and together they pushed the shorts down off his hips; the waistband caught on his cock until it bounced free, close to Alec's mouth.

Brant couldn't say "no" even if he wanted to, so he didn't say anything.

Alec wiped the cream off his hands onto a towel and reached toward Brant's cock. He smiled and met Brant's gaze again.

As Alec's fingers grazed his cock with electrifying reverberations, everything else fell away. The deal, his doubts about Alec's motivations, the problems with AK, even Ellie's meddling.

Nipples hard and tight, breaths shallow, Brant closed his eyes and focused on the one part of his body that hadn't been affected by sunscreen. He heard Alec's breath catching, smelled him, felt the heat of his body.

He concentrated on Alec's firm, knowing grasp but he couldn't shut his mind off completely and let his body take over. Doubts shattered the pleasure of Alec's touch.

What was he doing? He had no idea who Alec really was, where the ambitious dealmaker left off and the real man began. Brant needed to know.

"You know this is really, really inappropriate." Brant barely whispered the words, hoping Alec might not even hear.

"I suppose it is. I should stop, shouldn't I?"

"You should." Brant hoped like hell Alec would *not* stop.

Alec loosened his grip and Brant's senses focused in on the pain enveloping the rest of his body.

"But...," Brant started. He didn't know how to ask without actually *asking*. Did Alec really want this, or was he simply playing along for the sake of a big bonus check and a promotion?

"But?" Alec echoed, his expression bordering on hopeful.

"You'd practically be in breach of contract if you stopped now."

"Was this in the contract?" Alec's tone was playful as his hand hovered millimeters away from Brant's aching cock.

"An implied contract, which you've already begun to uh, perform." The legal terminology was never more appropriate Brant thought.

"Are you getting all legal on my ass?" Another daring smirk from Alec.

"You have no idea how much I'd love to, but I'm not sure I'm up to that much exertion at the moment."

"Then we better stick with the original plan, and save that for another time?"

"God, yes."

"Do you want to sit down, maybe on the edge of the bed?"

"Yeah." Brant sat and Alec settled on the floor between his knees. He wrapped a hand around Brant's cock and moved up and down a few times, trying different types of movement and gauging Brant's reactions. Then he licked his lips and leaned in, opening his mouth less than an inch from the dripping head of Brant's cock.

Brant shivered with anticipation, longing for the soft lips, the damp heat, the flick of a tongue. Alec had such a beautiful mouth. Brant had noticed that first day in his office, watching his lips as he spoke, and again as Alec chatted in French with the kids.

Now, that mouth was about to offer him pure pleasure.

"This isn't how I wanted it ..., wanted you," Brant began.

Alec stopped, his lips only millimeters away from Brant. He glanced up, eyes dark, pupils wide. Brant could see the bulge at Alec's crotch. A look of disappointment flashed across Alec's features.

"You don't like this? Then let me know what you want."

"Come here." Suddenly Brant felt more vulnerable and open than ever. He tugged at Alec's hand, bringing him to sit on the bed. Alec's hand moved to his own waistband and began to unbutton his shorts but Brant stopped him. Without speaking he moved his mouth to Alec's, letting his lips just brush against them. Damn, they were even softer than he'd imagined. He did it again, this time with slightly more pressure and Alec let out a surprised sigh.

They kissed, their bodies barely touching, Alec avoided any pressure on Brant's sensitive skin. Soon Alec's hand snaked its way to Brant's cock, and Brant let his knees fall open as Alec stroked and squeezed. Brant finished unbuttoning Alec's shorts, freeing his cock and taking it in his hand, thumbing the slit, slick with pre-come. He could feel Alec shudder, and he used Alec's breath and sounds to determine what he liked.

After only a few strokes from Brant, Alec slipped off the bed to again kneel between

Brant's knees, forcing Brant to let go of him. Brant watched as finally Alec's lips encircled his cock, his fervent tongue exploring its contours, sending jolts of pure sensation to every nerve ending in Brant's body. He leaned back, propping himself on his elbows and leaving Alec in control.

Alec knew what he was doing: bringing Brant to the edge several times before easing off, reducing pressure or slowing his motions. Alec's own little moans let Brant know he enjoyed giving this pleasure. When finally Brant could hold out no longer, he put a hand on Alec's shoulder, then on Alec's jaw line. Their eyes met, and Brant struggled to keep his eyes open as Alec caught Brant's release, to watch as Alec's own pleasure became evident in the brightness of his eyes.

Alec swallowed, then licked along Brant's cock, tickling around his balls, sucking each one gently, before he planted a last kiss on Brant's softening shaft.

As the last shudders of orgasm wracked his body, Brant leaned down to kiss Alec again. He hoped Alec hadn't done this for the wrong reasons.

"Your turn," Brant half-whispered, still not in full control of his voice. "I know it's nearly Christmas, but you can't really enjoy giving more than receiving."

"But I did."

Alec's swollen cock and peaked nipples told Brant he wouldn't be satisfied with stopping now. He stood, let Brant slip his shorts all the way off his body, and stepped out of them; then Brant got Alec to lie on the bed and lay down next him.

"Maybe just your hand...," Alec said when Brant's mouth moved in the direction of Alec's cock.

"Okay." Could Alec be that much of a bottom he didn't want a blow job? Brant wanted to taste Alec's cock even more now, but he wouldn't, unless Alec wanted it.

As he stroked Alec, Brant planted kisses along his hip or the inside of Alec's thigh, occasionally licking a stripe. Alec was born in Switzerland, but he was circumcised, which made Brant curious. Had the Switzerland story been made up? He focused on Alec's cock again and when he knew Alec was close, lavished just a few tiny kisses on his cock. Alec shuddered and moaned, tangling one hand through Brant's hair, unconsciously pulling tighter as he came. Brant liked it, the only real sign Alec had lost any degree of control and let his body take over.

Brant didn't manage to catch everything in his hand and come dripped down his fingers and onto Alec's belly. He bent low to lick the taut abs clean, letting the sandy trail of hairs tickle his tongue.

Alec unwound his fingers from Brant's hair with a self-conscious apology, but he continued carding his fingers through the strands. Brant laid his head on Alec's side and enjoyed the intimacy.

"Between you and that cream, I feel so much better."

"Glad to help."

"You're a regular Santa's Little Elf. Or not so little."

Alec let out a sweet, shy laugh that surprised Brant. So far he'd been so outgoing and cocky, but Brant liked seeing there was more to the man. And he couldn't wait to dig below the surface.

EM Lynley

CHAPTER ELEVEN

Christmas Day

Brant woke up before the first rays of sunlight pierced the darkness as rain pattered softly against the window. After the recent unseasonable sunshine, Christmas began with the islands' more typical winter wind and driving rain, but it wouldn't dampen the celebration.

Ellie's cream had done wonders, and he felt no trace of discomfort or pain. Instead, he felt a pain of a different sort. As he had their first night together, Brant watched as Alec slept, listening to the rhythm of his breath, and the occasional soft sigh. Alec shifted position and the sheet covering him slipped down toward his hips, exposing his flat stomach and navel, with just the hint of sandy trail leading lower.

Brant wanted Alec more than ever. But even though he knew Alec wanted him back, it wasn't quite right yet. Alec's motivation was still a mystery.

It was the damn deal. It had gotten them together in the first place, but now it hovered between them. If it were up to Brant, he'd forget about Turner Foods to concentrate on getting to know Alec, and enjoying the time with him.

But Alec *needed* the deal. If Brant backed out, Alec would be fucked, much more literally than anything they were about to do. Alec would lose his job, and Brant couldn't let that happen. But he needed to know if that were the only reason Alec was being so accommodating.

Then Alec opened his eyes.

"How long have you been watching me?"

Brant didn't try to deny it, but felt heat flush through his entire body. Alec rolled closer, this time the sheet slipped down. Alec's erection revealed he was at least as interested in taking things to the next level as Brant.

"Alec," Brant began but Alec leaned in for a kiss causing Brant's body to overrule his brain. He'd be a fool to stop again, now. They could sort everything out later on. What did it matter if Alec was there for different reasons than Brant was? They could both get what they wanted; it happened all the time, in business and out.

Alec's hands burned trails down and across Brant's skin, his mouth hot and demanding, teeth softly grazing first one nipple, then the other, moving down then back up for another deep kiss that left no doubt Alec reciprocated Brant's desire.

Without breaking their kiss, Alec stroked the length of Brant's cock with a firm touch, driving Brant even wilder. He let his hands and mouth explore every inch of Alec he could reach, as the first rays of morning crept in through rain-spattered windows.

Loud, joyous shrieks of childish glee disrupted their ardor.

The kids were up and running around already, banging on the door and proclaiming "*Joyeux Noël!* And Merry Christmas, sleepyheads!" through Brant and Alec's door, making any further intimacy between them impossible or at the very least, imprudent.

"Be down in a minute," Brant shouted back, and heard the voices trail away downstairs. "Merry Christmas," Brant whispered as he kissed his way down Alec's chest, but Alec gave him a resigned look and a perfect imitation of Henri's Gallic shrug.

"*Joyeux Noël*, Brant." Alec grinned and sat up.

"Don't I at least get a French kiss with that?"

"Can I give you a rain check? You know they'll be running in here if we don't show up soon enough. No lock on the door."

Brant knew Alec was right. He hopped out of bed and took the briefest of showers, washing away all trace of the cream and of their abortive lovemaking, then he threw on a pair of shorts and a T-shirt, the best of the meager selection of clothing AK had left him.

"You are not going to wear that for Christmas are you?" Alec already sounded like a boyfriend, but Brant was in such a good mood the mild admonishment only made him laugh.

Alec was wearing chinos and a short-sleeved silk blend shirt in a pale melon-green that somehow brought out the gold halos in his eyes.

"Did I mention AK only packed beach-bum attire for me?"

"I'm such a bitch!" Alec teased, then turned serious again. "No wonder you didn't want him following you here. You're close enough to my size, feel free." Alec nodded toward his suitcase.

Brant hesitated. Despite their night together, wearing another man's clothes seemed so much more intimate than what had already passed between them.

"Here, let me choose something." Alec's eyes twinkled as he went through the clothing and after some moments selected an outfit.

Brant liked the amount of thought Alec put into the choice, making the gesture so much more intimate and personal.

Five minutes later they arrived downstairs, Brant now wearing a soft cranberry shirt and khakis, all with Alec's personal seal of approval.

"Don't you two look just like Christmas? Green and red." Ellie cheerfully kissed first Brant then Alec on the cheek. "Merry Christmas!"

Henri handed them steaming mugs of spiced apple cider. "There's champagne, too, but let's save that till at least nine."

"*Now* can we start?" Sunday, today in head-to-toe bright-Christmas green, let out an award-winning sigh of impatience.

Next to her, Jenner waited quietly, probably knowing as soon as Sunday got her way, he'd benefit without any effort. Smart kid.

Alec and Brant sat on the couch, while Ellie and Henri sat in chairs, everyone watching the kids crouching on the floor in front of the tree.

"Sure honey. Roll to see who goes first." Ellie handed Sunday a large stuffed toy in the shape of a die. "Otherwise there's a ...scene," she explained in a soft whisper to Alec.

Thankfully, for peace in the Lafontaine household, Sunday got the lowest score. "I'm going to open one from Uncle Brant first."

Brant hoped like hell he'd made the right choices. If there was one task he'd enjoyed, it was shopping for the twins. He and AK had spent a lovely day, playing with half the toys at FAO Schwartz and acting like kids themselves. The day had ended with Brant buying a watch for AK, which cost more than all the kids' presents combined. He shook off the memory and focused on enjoying Christmas, here and now. With Alec and not AK.

Sunday chose the largest box of the half dozen or so Brant had for her and ripped the paper off in half a second flat.

"What's a W-I-I?" she asked after looking over the box. "Computer games?"

"Cool!" Jenner reached for the box and Sunday frowned.

"It's a Wii— pronounced 'wee.' And it's for both of you," Brant said, his own excitement fading at Ellie's disapproving furrowed brow. "There's a bunch of different games in some of the other boxes, like tennis or singing. You use the handles like this." He stood and demonstrated. "Plus one so you could learn to play the piano, Sunday."

"I wanted to learn guitar." Sunday's shoulders sagged as she surveyed the smaller boxes, clearly not expecting anything better.

"Okay. Cancel delivery of the piano," Brant said so softly only Alec seemed to notice. The accompanying elbow squeeze surprised Brant, but it brightened his mood more than he should have let it.

"At least it's not a Red Ryder BB gun," Alec pointed out, making Ellie and Brant laugh.

The kids and Henri looked confused, so Alec added. "I'll show you later, after you open the rest of the gifts."

"What other games are there, Uncle B?" Jenner asked politely.

Brant launched into an explanation of Wii and pointed out which gift box held the rest of the age-appropriate Wii games, with assistance from Alec who disarmed Ellie's displeasure by explaining the fitness applications. Thank goodness he was there to back Brant up, though the pressure from his thigh against Brant's was far too distracting.

"Thanks, Uncle B." Sunday hugged him but she didn't seem as thrilled as he'd hoped. He knew next to nothing about kids. Ellie had given him a list of suggested gifts and price limits, but he'd strayed a bit. He hoped the rest of his gifts didn't fall as flat as this one had. Being filthy rich didn't mean he could just buy love even from his family, and he didn't want it any other way.

But Sunday loved the charm bracelet he'd chosen for her along with iPads for both kids and a high-quality set of paints and brushes for Jenner.

"They're from Alec too. He didn't think he should sign the gift cards before he met you."

"Thanks, Uncle Alec." Both kids wrapped their arms around Alec who hugged back just as heartily, throwing Brant a surprised but grateful grin.

"I have a few surprises left," Alec said and pulled some items from behind the couch. He handed one to each kid.

Sunday was thrilled with a knitting kit and Jenner couldn't let go of the Harry Potter LEGO set. Brant was most stunned of all to see their response.

"Alec, I'm sorry we don't have anything for you," Henri said while the kids were distracted. "We didn't know you'd be joining us."

"Don't worry at all. It's enough of a treat to be here with your family. Thank you for having me."

"It's our pleasure," Ellie said and hugged Alec.

"Well, *ma petite* Sunday, I have one last gift for you," Henri said as he stood. He went to the den and returned with a long box, adorned with a large green bow affixed to one side.

"I already got everything I wanted," she said but Brant noticed she gave a forlorn little glance at his failed piano software. He felt awful, but apparently Henri had kept something in reserve.

Sunday opened the box, letting out a delighted shriek as she uncovered a black guitar case. Inside lay a shiny new acoustical guitar.

Henri threw a Gallic shrug toward Brant but he wasn't disappointed to be one-upped at all.

Sunday pulled the guitar out of the case and gave a few tentative strums. "Thank you so much, Papa! Can you teach me to play it?"

"We'll get you some lessons, *chérie.* I don't know how to play."

Sunday looked nearly as disappointed as before. Her much-longed-for gift seemed useless and boring now.

"Let me see," Alec said, settling himself on the floor next to Sunday. "I used to play a little. Maybe I can still . . ." He held out a hand and Sunday, torn between fondling her new possession and trusting Alec, an exciting but very new friend, eventually gave in and handed it over.

Alec strummed a few chords, adjusted a couple of knobs to tune it, then launched into a familiar song:

"It's not easy being green," he sang.

"Ohmigod! I looooove Kermit!" Sunday was jelly at Alec's feet. Again.

Alec threw Brant a "however could I guess" glance, and continued singing. Everyone joined in gleefully. Alec charmed them all further by even doing a verse in

French, clearly ad-libbed based on the occasional pause and knotted brows. But even Henri was practically rolling on the floor with whatever Alec came up with.

Even though Brant barely understood the words, he loved every minute of it. As Alec played the strings of Sunday's new guitar, he pulled strings in Brant's heart.

He knew this was the real Alec, a genuinely kind and caring person, generous with his wit and his body, someone Brant wanted more than ever to spend time with. As his regard grew, Brant reminded himself that Alec was here for the deal first and foremost. Anything between them was strictly for show and temporary, no matter how enjoyable.

They spent the rest of the day competing in cut-throat rounds of Wii tennis and bowling, passing new gifts around and generally stuffing themselves with another impressive assortment of delights from Henri.

Alec had also brought some Blu-Ray discs of holiday classic films, including his own family favorite, *A Christmas Story*, and he introduced the kids and Henri to the legend of the Red Ryder BB gun.

"Thank you, Alec, for starting a new tradition for us," Henri said. He seemed to enjoy the film as much as the kids.

Brant hadn't seen it since he and Ellie had been kids and it was an enjoyable blast from the past and everyone was exhausted from laughing so hard.

"It makes me appreciate the beach a lot more." Sunday had shivered whenever the kids went outside to play in the snow.

After the film, Jenner sat on the couch in his own little world, engrossed in a book on his brand-new iPad. Brant was surprised he hadn't started working on the LEGO set, then realized he didn't want to share it with Sunday. The boy reminded him of himself at that age, except in his distinct lack of competition with his overbearing sister.

All day, Brant found himself recalling his early morning kisses with Alec. A gesture or word from Alec would have him longing to be with him again, to finish what they'd started. The spark between them was brighter than ever and they shared smoldering glances when they thought no one would notice. When Alec's hand or leg brushed against him, Brant's entire body was on fire again, not with the forgotten pain of his allergy, but with renewed desire he couldn't yet act on.

It was almost torture, watching Alec pop a morsel of fruit or pastry in his mouth, imagining an entirely different and more pleasurable scenario.

Finally, dusk descended and with the day's early start, the kids were exhausted well before their usual bedtime. They went to bed without battle while the adults enjoyed the bottles of vintage Clicquot Brant had brought.

"I can't remember a better Christmas since we were about ten." Brant breathed a sigh of relief it had turned out so well after an iffy start.

"So what did you two get each other?" Ellie asked.

Brant glanced at Alec next to him on the couch, their thighs barely touching, but just enough connection to keep the spark high without being too obvious in front of Ellie and Henri.

Brant's gifts for AK hadn't been in the suitcase, and even if they had been, he wouldn't have put them under the tree. It would have been inappropriate to give them to Alec, even for show. After little more than a day together, it was clear Alec's personality and tastes could hardly be more different from AK's--understated and elegant, based on what he'd brought with him. Ellie and Henri would realize just how shallow AK had been by what he'd wanted, but Brant didn't want them to think poorly of Alec.

"I have something upstairs for Alec," he said, noticing Alec looked appropriately embarrassed by the topic.

"Me too," Alec murmured, gazing into Brant's eyes so convincingly Brant wasn't sure how much was an act.

"Well, let's not keep the lovebirds from exchanging their private gifts," Ellie said and shooed them off the couch in the direction of the stairs.

When Brant slipped his hand into Alec's as they headed for the stairs, it seemed the most natural thing in the world.

* * * *

As soon as the door closed, their mouths came together in a kiss, at first tentative and gentle, then with less restraint.

Brant wondered how he'd kept his hands off Alec the whole day, with memories of lovemaking the night before flashing through his mind at the most inopportune moments. He moaned softly against Alec's lips, felt Alec's arousal mirror his own.

But Brant wasn't ready to give in to temptation just yet.

"When did you get those gifts?" he asked.

"I had some time before my flight left. I didn't even know if you'd see me, so it was just on a whim I collected a few things."

"The knitting kit and the LEGOs?" Brant was impressed that Alec managed to choose such appropriate gifts without the agonizing thought he'd put into his selections.

"I cheated. I asked my brothers what they got for their kids around those ages. I took a gamble that a girl living on a tropical island would like knitting as much as one in Chicago." Alec shrugged.

The fact Alec had asked his own family made the choices more meaningful and personal, even though he'd never met the twins.

"I suspect you could have given them lumps of coal and they would have loved it. You have a great way with kids."

"It's much easier when they aren't your kids. Or so my siblings tell me. But I think they adored your gifts too."

Brant felt a little upstaged by Alec. Usually he was the twins' hero when he visited, but for a change he got to see them from Ellie and Henri's point of view: taking pleasure in their enjoyment, no matter who brought it about.

Since the moment they'd met, Alec had turned Brant's world upside down and he felt richer for the experience in a way that had nothing to do with money. It was time to thank Alec in a more private and personal way.

"I think I know what you've got for me," Alec said as he ran his hands under Brant's shirt, fingernails creating trails of fire.

"You do?" Brant was curious. Did he mean resuming where they'd left off so many long hours earlier? He reached under Alec's shirt and teased a nipple, felt it harden, then went for the other.

"A signature?"

Brant's heart lurched. He thought they'd moved past their original arrangement. "Is that all you want from me?"

"No. But I was afraid to hope for more." Alec proved the point by pulling Brant's shirt over his head and tossing it aside.

"Good."

"Right now I only want to get to know you better." Alec began unbuttoning Brant's pants.

"After last night I think you know me better than most." Brant grinned, glad to bring the topic to a less serious and more personal level. The wonderful day and the Champagne-fueled glow had him craving Alec, how much he had wanted him all day.

"I want to know more than the surface. And more than just physically," Alec said.

"He says while undressing me."

"Good point." Alec slipped off his own shirt and pants. "At least now we're even." He lay down on the bed and held out an arm toward Brant.

"All right. What do you want to know?" Brant settled next to Alec, wondering where this was leading.

"What's the real story behind leaving med school?" Alec's expression held a mixture of hopefulness and wariness, in case this might be a difficult topic for Brant.

"It's complicated."

"I know that's what you told the journalist who wrote the *Forbes* feature—and nearly everyone else who's ever asked—but I'd really like to know. No matter what or why. Did you lose a patient?"

"Actually, it was because of a patient who lived. Losing a patient is not the worst thing." Not many people knew the whole story, but Alec already knew so much about him as a person and not just as an image. "It's much worse when you fuck up and the guy lives, only his life isn't normal because of something you did."

Alec reached out to place a hand on Brant's wrist. "Hey, it's okay. You don't have to tell me."

Brant gave a pained half-laugh. "Actually, there's a happy ending. It's the beginning and the middle that were rough." He sighed. "I was an intern, done with med school, had the 'M.D.' after my name and felt pretty cocky. I rushed through a procedure in the ER just to win a bet I could handle more patients than another doc. The patient ended up partially paralyzed, and if I'd been more careful, he would have recovered completely."

"But he lived, right? That must have made up for whatever you did."

"Not so cut-and-dried. I felt responsible and when he finally woke up, I confessed everything; the bet, my carelessness. I thought for sure there'd be a lawsuit. He agreed I was a lousy doc, because my heart clearly wasn't in it. He urged me to find something I wanted to do for the right reasons, and offered me a job."

"As what?"

"The guy happened to be Byron Voight."

"No kidding, that's how you met Voight? I knew he'd been your mentor, taken you under his wing and taught—" Alec stopped, suddenly embarrassed.

"Don't worry, I know you've read articles about me. You wouldn't be doing your job if you didn't."

Alec looked away suddenly, and the spell was broken. Brant had fucked up again. He'd brought business into what had been a personal conversation, a moment of bonding as equals.

"Is this just work for you, then, Brant?" Alec's voice had taken on a familiar tone, one Brant had heard from AK a million times. Hearing it now cut Brant to the core in a way AK never could. He leaned close and stroked Alec's hair, letting a finger trail down the back of his neck, feeling the muscles tighten under the smooth tanned skin.

"It's not *just* work. Right now, it's not work at all, but I do want to do the Turner deal with you. For you."

"Because I came halfway around the world for it?"

"No, because it's a good deal. I'm in bed with you because you're hot *and* you came halfway around the world for it." Brant laughed, and thankfully Alec joined in.

"I suppose letting your sister think I was your boyfriend didn't hurt."

"Not once I realized what I'd miss out on if I didn't go along with your charade."

"You mean the deal or the sex?"

"Stop talking." Brant leaned in and covered Alec's mouth with his, enjoying the sensation as Alec kept talking through the kiss. When Brant reached down to gently tug at a nipple, Alec finally stopped talking, instead, moaning softly and opening up his posture to Brant. He reached into the nightstand drawer and retrieved lube and condoms, without saying a word.

Once Alec was ready, Brant rolled the condom on. He'd been thinking of this moment for at least the past twenty-four hours—no, in truth, since he'd first surprised Alec in his office, only a few days earlier. He wanted to be inside Alec, to feel and know him inside and out. But more than taking, Brant wanted to give himself to Alec.

Now it was Brant who hesitated in their thrice-interrupted lovemaking, hovering over Alec. He wanted Alec with every fiber of his being, more than ever after spending the day with this incredible man. But would it be crossing a line to sleep with him when he didn't understand Alec's full motivation?

"Hurry before the kids wake up again." Alec spread his legs wider and grabbed Brant's ass, pulling him down on top.

"You don't have to do this, Alec."

"You can't possibly think I'm pretending about how much I want you."

Brant looked at Alec, hard and ready beneath him, panting slightly, full lips parted. He couldn't hold back his own desire any longer unless Alec pushed him away.

Pressing against the ring of muscle, easing himself in slowly, Brant let Alec's body grip him tight, make way for him, welcome him in. Brant heard a sharp intake of breath, a little gasp of pleasure, and realized it was his own. Below him, Alec's gaze was fixed on his, Alec's mouth, those obscenely beautiful lips, parted and the tip of his tongue flicked out to glide along a lower lip. Something about that got Brant even hotter, and he pushed the rest of the way home, with Alec clenching and shuddering.

Again, everything about Alec was so much more than Brant had a right to expect. How utterly exhilarating to be here with someone who engaged Brant's mind and soul as well as his body. Overpowering emotion took Brant by surprise and he gulped oxygen to keep himself centered.

After recovering some degree of equilibrium Brant let physical desire rule again. He alternated quick and slow movements, deep and shallow, thrusts and long strokes, and eventually, they found a rhythm. Alec's hands seemed to be everywhere, stroking his shoulder or back, tickling his balls, or gripping his hair— apparently Alec's little habit. They shifted positions, moving around the bed, both wanting more, harder, deeper but knowing the more they took the sooner it would be over, and they fell back into a more languorous rhythm.

Their bodies heated and slick, Brant didn't know where he ended and Alec began, and he didn't care. When they both finally came, they lay locked together, neither willing to let the other go, panting in each other's ears, kissing mouths, faces, throats, held together by the glue of their sweat and release. Then finally still, they embraced while their heartbeats slowed and the world around them came back into focus.

* * * *

Afterward, as they lay together, Brant listened to Alec's soft breathing. He wondered whether Alec had experienced the same soul-shattering experience he had.

"Alec, do you want to show me those spreadsheets?" Business was the last thing on Brant's mind. He ached to lie in bed with Alec for days and explore everything about him: mind, body, and more.

"Now?" Alec's tone conveyed surprise. He rolled away and the absence of his heat chilled Brant, even in the tropical temperature of the room. "Were you thinking about that while we were …?" Alec's voice trailed off, but the unmistakable pain cut through Brant's afterglow.

"No. God, no." Brant shut his eyes, wishing he could take back the words. When he opened them again Alec stared at him with disbelief. "I was a little worried that might be what you were thinking. If that's why you're here."

"And you're not?" Alec's tone was accusatory.

"No, you know that."

"Oh, right, you're in bed with me because I'm your pretend boyfriend."

That hurt, but Brant deserved it. He had asked Alec to pretend for Ellie's sake and for his own.

"I'm not pretending either." Brant's stomach knotted. What was he saying? It was how he felt but he couldn't believe he'd revealed this to Alec.

"Yeah, that definitely was genuine sex." Alec's glare sputtered and turned into a smile, and he let out one of those genuine laughs that melted Brant's resolve so many times already.

Brant relaxed and joined in. "I didn't just mean the sex. I meant more. I'd like more."

"More sex?" Alec's playfulness had returned. "Already?"

"More than sex. From you." Brant decided to lay the cards out, something he'd never do in business; he was so out of practice of telling anyone the whole truth about anything, especially himself. "I wish we didn't have this deal clouding the situation between us."

"And your sister?"

"Right. That's my fault. I was afraid of either offending you or scaring you off, or possibly both. I'm not particularly good at personal relationships when they aren't about business."

"You didn't really explain what happened with the actor, but I'm going out on limb . . . communication problems had something to do with it?"

"We talked."

"Talked? Or negotiated?"

Brant remained silent. Alec understood AK better than he had. They hadn't *discussed* as much as dealt. Simply "You want this and I want that." There had never been much "we" between them. Brant hadn't noticed until too late.

"If you ever leave finance, you could go into psychology." Brant traced a finger across Alec's shoulder and down one freckled, muscular arm.

"I'll keep that in mind, especially if I need a new job in January,"

"Don't worry about your job. I won't let you down. I'd do the deal just to help you, if necessary."

"You'd invest a billion dollars to keep me from losing my job?"

"Sure, why not?"

"And what would you expect in return?" Alec grinned, but Brant knew he wasn't entirely joking.

"Nothing more than you want to give. I just need to know whether you're interested in me for more than this deal, or have I just completely humiliated myself in front of you. Again."

"So you still want to see those spreadsheets?" Alec traced a finger along Brant's cheek and planted a soft kiss on the corner of his mouth. The gestures were gentle and intimate, and Brant hoped that was Alec's answer.

"You show me yours and I'll show you mine."

"Always negotiating." Alec's whisper was low and even in Brant's sated state it went directly to his core.

"Alec, it's not always bad to find out what the other guy wants, is it?"

"What if I want you to stop talking?"

Brant was ready to give in without any further negotiations.

Their mouths met, at first hard and needy, but as the kiss deepened, it slowed and sweetened. Brant didn't want to rush through anything with Alec tonight. But he didn't need words to communicate or to fully understand everything Alec wanted to tell him. Their bodies spoke and listened, not yet perfectly in tune, but experimenting with a touch, a look, a kiss, a moan.

Later, when Brant pushed into Alec's slick heat again, he realized everything had changed since the previous night. The connection was stronger than he'd ever felt with anyone, far beyond the physical. The man intrigued him, ambitious and calculating one minute, and entertaining Sunday and Jenner on the guitar the next.

Brant wanted to get to know Alec, and just fucking him for a few days on vacation would be eminently unsatisfying.

CHAPTER TWELVE

December 26

Brant didn't think anything could top Christmas night with Alec, but their morning after absolutely did. After gentle and very quiet lovemaking, Alec and Brant showered, and then wandered downstairs a little after eight. The kids were wide awake: Jenner reading a book, and Sunday jabbing him with fallen pine needles.

"Mom's gone to the hospital, and Dad's at the resort," Sunday announced, poking Jenner with each word. Apparently he was immune and just slapped her hand away every three or four jabs, preferring to concentrate on his book—one of the Lord of the Rings series, though the title was in French so Brant didn't bother trying to figure out which.

"You guys must be hungry." Jenner grinned and put his iPad down before giving Brant and Alec a forlorn look that reminded Brant of a puppy.

Had anyone but a ten-year-old boy made the comment, Brant would have suspected a dirty joke, but Jenner just didn't make those sorts of jokes. He was a very literal boy. And a very hungry boy. He had been talking about himself, Brant realized.

"Did your dad leave anything for breakfast?" Alec asked, taking a step toward the kitchen. "I would kill for some of his fabulous coffee. Smells like he made some before he left." Alec sniffed the air visibly and his eyes lit up, then he headed toward the heavenly aroma.

Truth was, they *had* worked up an appetite, and despite the spectacular Christmas feast, Brant's stomach rumbled at the thought of another of Henri's sumptuous breakfasts.

"Nope. He said you'd feed us."

"Oh." Brant was no cook and said as much.

"You don't have to cook, Uncle B," Jenner said brightly. He hopped off the couch, grabbing Brant's arm and pulling him toward the kitchen. That puppy analogy seemed more apt than ever.

Once inside, Jenner stood on tippy toes in front of one of the cupboards and tried to open the door. Alec, sipping coffee from a mug, opened the cabinet for him.

"Can we pleeeeease have Peanut Butter Crunchy Pops? Mom hardly *ever* lets us have those. They have the best prizes ever. A friend of mine once won a pony!" Jenner bounced in front of the cabinet, and Brant wondered if sugar would really be a good idea given the boy's already-high energy level.

"A pony? You're lying. You're such a lying liar. I'm telling Mom." Sunday added something in French, which Brant didn't even want to translate. Alec's chuckle gave him a pretty good idea what it meant.

"Please Uncle B?" Jenner ignored Sunday's insults.

Jenner's breakfast of choice was interesting, given that the cereal was one of Turner Foods' bands. But before Brant could respond, Alec pulled the box down and handed it to Jenner. Sunday, who had been watching silently ran up and grabbed the box away. She ran to the other side of the kitchen, opened the box and jammed her hand inside, rooting around for the prize promised on the front of the box.

"Hey, Sunday, that's not how it's done," Brant said. Actually that was how it had been done when he and Ellie were kids, unless an adult was around to prevent carnage.

"Jenner, get bowls and milk, and whoever gets the prize in their bowl owns it. No one digs out the prize."

"That's not how we did it when I was a kid," Alec said, helping Jenner with the milk. "Dad used to get boxes of Crunchy Pops sent from the States. But the three of us fought over the prizes like mad dogs. Even if the prize fell in someone else's bowl, we'd argue. Eventually my mom told him to stop getting them."

"Your mom wouldn't let you have Peanut Butter Crunchy Pops? How mean!" Sunday sounded sorry for Alec's apparently deprived childhood.

"Actually, Dad's solution was for each of us to have our own box."

"Smart guy." Brant set bowls and spoons out on the table. Too bad there was only one box of Crunchy Pops in the house.

Sunday sat, letting the men do all the work. Her lower lip stuck out in an exaggerated pout and Brant knew she was trying to figure out whether to take the first or last bowl. That's what he always did.

Brant decided to head off any chance for argument. "OK, Alec goes first, then me, then Jenner. Sunday, you're last."

"What kind of stupid order is that?" Sunday complained.

"Alphabetical," Jenner replied with a know-it-all smirk and handed the box politely to Alec.

"Jen-*nerd*. I told you!"

Alec gently poured himself a bowl, clearly not wanting to get the prize. Brant glanced at the box to see what all the fighting was about and decided the prize was worth all the hubbub: a super-cool-looking spy decoder ring that had barely changed in appearance since his own childhood. He sort of even hoped he'd get it, but ended up with only a bowl full of peanut-butter scented yellow balls that smelled even better than he remembered. He'd loved these as a kid but hadn't had them since med school probably, when most days he barely even had time for a handful of dry cereal out of a box.

Sunday's gaze shot bad juju at Jenner as he smacked a palm against the bottom of the box, attempting to coax the prize into his bowl. She whooped very impolitely at his failure, though her own attempt to finesse the shy prize into her bowl was equally unsuccessful.

For a few moments the only sounds were the four of them slurping and crunching away until Brant's curiosity got the better of him. He peeked into the nearly empty box to discover there was no prize nestled in the peanut-buttery dust at the bottom.

"No prize in a brand new box? That's *such* a rip-off!" Sunday sounded a lot more like the kids in New York when her parents weren't around, Brant noticed. At least she hadn't said "freaking rip-off," or worse.

"You know this box has hardly changed since I was a kid. You'd think Turner would bring it into the twenty-first century by now. The cereal's good, but the box looks so old-fashioned."

"Maybe they're trying to appeal to the moms. Nostalgia, or *retro* as they call it now," Alec replied.

"That would explain a lot. Thing is, nowadays, even though moms do the shopping, kids drive the purchases."

"Ohmigod. I'm stuck at a table of *three* big, fat nerds!"

Sunday's indignant remark had them all laughing. Brant nearly snorted milk. That would really have been embarrassing in front of Alec. They'd gotten close, especially after the previous night, but he needed to keep some semblance of dignity, even with ten-year-olds around.

Sunday seemed to settle down after no one got the prize and they discussed what to do that day. They consulted Ellie's list and chose snorkeling off one of the sandy *motu* to the north of the island, where there were silky beaches, Technicolor coral, and unforgettable views of both Taha'a and Bora Bora to the north. The weather had improved, and they decided to sail again, rather than take the motor launch, especially given the delicate nature of the reef.

* * * *

The wind was perfect for the journey out and they anchored off the *motu*, ferrying dry towels and lunch to the beach in the small rubber dinghy they'd brought along.

Alec found himself enjoying the day but dreading the business discussion Brant had planned for after lunch.

They snorkeled off the beach, spotting dozens of brightly color fish darting around, and a few large, dark rays, gliding menacingly, though the kids assured Alec they were harmless. He wished he could take photos of the gorgeous sea life, but nothing would replace seeing everything for real. Or that it was Brant who introduced him to such peace and beauty under the surface.

Even with the kids the experience was surprisingly romantic. He and Brant swam at their own pace, pointing and smiling as they showed their discoveries to the other. Their hands and arms brushed together in the warm water and Alec had to calm his pounding heart for fear he'd drown.

Lunch on the beach was quiet and subdued, everyone ravenous after the exertions of snorkeling.

Alec found himself dreading the business discussion Brant had planned after lunch and ate slowly, listlessly.

"Uncle B, can we go down the beach a ways?" Jenner asked, surprising Alec by taking the initiative.

"Sure, just stay in sight of us. If I can't see you, I'm going to pack up and leave." Brant winked at Alec, but Jenner looked worried.

"Yes, don't worry."

"Have fun," Alec said, but he didn't want them to go.

The twins ran off down the beach to entertain themselves while Brant cozied up to Alec on the blanket.

He wished they could enjoy a romantic cuddle, but time was running out, and Big Ben expected results. He'd emailed Alec twice on Christmas wondering why he hadn't closed the damn deal yet. He'd also forwarded some of Schrader's additional research they'd pulled of his computer after he'd been booted out.

Alec had glanced over the material while Brant had showered the night before. Now he dreaded bringing it up, but Brant had asked about the Turner pension plans.

Once the kids were out of earshot, Alec steeled himself. He pulled his laptop out of the waterproof bag and pulled up the spreadsheets they'd joked about the night before.

"I've been going over some of the figures. This balance sheet's beautiful." Alec let out a low whistle, trying to conjure up enthusiasm. "I can see why you didn't have to think twice about this deal. What was holding it up?"

"Schrader hadn't provided me with all the data I needed. Are there any notes about the pension plan?"

"Yes. Big Ben found them on a flash drive in Hank's desk and forwarded the data to me yesterday."

"Yesterday was Christmas. You weren't kidding when you said he really had a hard-on for getting this deal closed."

"I'm wondering why Schrader didn't follow up with you. The relevant correspondence with Turner Foods is dated two months ago." Schrader had always seemed good at following directions, even if he hadn't had much originality when it came to engineering deals. "After the Dubs and the senior partners, Schrader had been at Three Dub the longest. Maybe they had a soft spot for him or something." He paused, then he and Brant locked gazes, they laughed and shook their heads. "Nah."

Not many soft spots on Wall Street, except in a few heads after they'd been kicked out of what they'd thought were comfortable jobs. Like Alec, maybe.

He couldn't figure out why, but Linton seemed to be dragging the whole thing out far longer than necessary. He was loathe to remind Brant he needed this signed, sealed and delivered by December 31, but he acted as if time didn't matter at all; he hadn't really seemed to want this deal until last night.

Not that Alec hadn't enjoyed every moment he spent here. Brant's family had treated him like royalty and he loved the kids. Sharing a bed with Brant hadn't exactly been a hardship. Despite his usual rule of not sleeping with clients, Alec hadn't been able to resist Brant.

The problem was, now that Brant had committed to the deal, for Alec's sake, Alec didn't want him to go through with it. The new information from Schrader's flash drive put everything into a new perspective, and if Brant went through with the deal, Alec wasn't so sure he would have any respect, much less any more personal emotion for Brant Linton.

"So did the flash drive contain the research on the pension plan?"

Alec pretended to page through until he got to those figures. "Oh yeah, I see. Over funded. You could pull the excess cash out right away. Is that what you intended?" But Brant had intended something else, and Alec held his breath to see how he would respond.

"I asked Schrader to scour the contracts and determine whether we can reduce benefits to the current retirees or amend the terms for employees who haven't yet retired. That would be a cherry on top of the icing on the cake, though. Most companies have clauses where you can dig into the pot of pension gold during times of financial distress. The question is how deep we can excavate at Turner. It should be part of standard due diligence to look for it."

Alec found Schrader's notes detailed and meticulous. "Looks like you can cut benefits, if revenue and profits fall beneath specific levels for three consecutive quarters," he summarized for Brant.

"Didn't they fall below those thresholds?"

"Yes, for at least the last six quarters. But Turner never implemented the pension cuts. They could have avoided operating losses if they'd used the money for improvements."

"What were they thinking? That pension was running them into the ground." Brant leaned over Alec's shoulder to peer at the screen, shifting position until he found one that didn't have a glare.

Alec handed the laptop over to Brant, watching him flip through screens as he worked figures in his head. Turner Foods could only afford the necessary improvements if they cut benefits, but they hadn't and they were nearly out of business.

Now, Brant and his greedy cohorts would buy it up, unlock the piggy bank and spend the pension money. It was foolproof, pure profit, and completely legal. Turner Foods had been around forever, and had hundreds of retired employees drawing pensions. Even a small cutback in benefits would have given the company a much-needed financial boost.

The benefits could be repaid within a few years of increased profitability. But some retirees would have suffered in the short term. Now even more would suffer because Brant would likely cut benefit levels to the absolute minimum, squeezing out every ounce of profit.

Suddenly, Alec wasn't sure this deal was such a good thing after all. Those employees and pensioners would get notices in January, after a lovely holiday break to find out they couldn't pay the bills for the Christmas they just celebrated.

Most of Alec's holiday cheer had seeped away just thinking about it. He'd been such a fool, letting himself be caught up in the physical and emotional excitement of being with Brant. He'd fallen under the man's spell so easily. Why hadn't he just kept the attraction physical and not let the charm dull his normally sharp mind?

"So what do you think, Alec?"

"Think? About what?" Alec was confused. Brant had all but committed to the deal, so what did he need Alec's opinion on? In fact, Brant probably didn't want to know what he was thinking about the deal.

Linton's *modus operandi* had just become crystal clear to Alec, and he didn't like what he saw. He didn't know if he wanted to be involved in breaking up Turner Foods so Brant Linton could buy another boat or plane or island.

So far Alec's projects had been operating mergers or acquisitions, never before had he worked on a dissolution deal. He'd discovered the pensions weren't the only cuts Schrader had researched. Alec hadn't mentioned the results, but Brant was reading through Schrader's comments now, and he'd get the picture himself.

Could this be why Schrader had gotten pulled off the deal? Because *he'd* dragged his feet and not Brant? Schrader was a decent guy; Alec doubted he liked cutting benefits to retirees or putting loyal, hard-working employees out of work. Especially at a well-loved company like Turner Foods. It wasn't exactly Mom's apple pie, but they made many products that had been used for generations.

Their own breakfast was a prime example: Turner Foods owned the company that made Peanut Butter Crunchy Pops.

"Should I?" Brant's voice cut through Alec's painful musings.

"Cut the benefit?"

"Yeah. I mean I *can*, and there's a minimum level of continuing benefits required even if the company's dissolved. But that just seems so *wrong*."

Had Alec heard Brant correctly? Was he really having doubts about milking every penny out of Turner Foods and its employees?

"You think the other counterparties would still do the deal if I don't wring every penny out of Turner?" Brant put the laptop down and stared at Alec, waiting for an answer.

Alec's brain stopped working for a moment. "I don't know. I guaranteed them a minimum rate of return, but do you think you could still beat it without cleaning out the pensions?"

"We'll need to crunch some more numbers. At the worst case, I can cover their shortfall out of my share of profits. Or I can just do the whole deal on my own. I'm not locked into a minimum ROI."

Alec nearly did a double take. He sat up and gathered his thoughts. It sounded like Brant wasn't willing to harm the Turner employees, and he'd even take the cut in his own profits. That was not at all what Alec had expected, but he liked what Brant was saying.

"So you don't want to cut the pensions?"

"The overfunding can certainly be put to much better use, especially given the low return on the pension portfolio. I suspect that's why they didn't take the money out sooner."

"I agree." It was precisely that prudence that made Turner so vulnerable to a takeover right now. "But that's low-hanging fruit and ..." Alec stopped.

"Go on. What were you thinking?"

Alec took a breath and glanced down the beach to where the twins were kicking water at each other and shouting taunts. His future rested on the next thing he said. Either he put his personal ethics aside and helped Brant destroy Turner Foods, or he said what he really thought. He could be ethical and unemployed. Either way, he knew he'd lost the flame that briefly brought them together.

"Assuming you're going to break up Turner Foods...." Alec fought for the right words.

"I guess we have been operating under that assumption, but it's not the only option, is it?" Brant pressed his lips together and inhaled slowly. "What if we don't? We could do just what you said, channel that safety cushion into the changes Turner really needs."

Alec's heart went wild again as he searched Brant's face for clues to what he was thinking. The way Brant quirked his mouth told Alec he'd made Brant reevaluate the options.

Now Alec felt a new level of respect and affection for Brant. He'd gotten a reputation as a real divide-and-conquer type, destroying companies. How many times had he actually given up a guaranteed profit to avoid hurting someone? That wasn't the sort of action Brant would want publicized or he'd damage his reputation and his effectiveness for future deals.

But maybe he wasn't such a monster after all.

"You know, Brant, I think with a few operational changes, upgrades to key equipment, and a more modern marketing program, it would be a snap to turn this company around. It wouldn't cost much. More than Turner wanted to spend, but for you . . ." Alec didn't know what prompted him to make the suggestion. Despite the unexpected softer side, Brant was still a corporate raider, a buyout specialist, not someone who owned and ran going concerns.

Brant cocked his head slightly and stared at Alec again, still silent. Alec's heart rate speeded up. Had he really fucked up with his suggestion?

"I feel like an idiot admitting it, but this morning at breakfast, I was thinking it's too bad that Turner Foods and products like the Crunchy Pops would be gone and another generation of kids wouldn't get to enjoy them, but ..., do you think it would really be that easy?"

Alec let out a long sigh of relief. This was something he knew how to do. He'd effected plenty of turnarounds. "As pie."

"This is your area of expertise, isn't it?"

Alec stared.

"I did my due diligence on you too." Brant's eyes lit up again. "How'd you end up on this deal in the first place?"

"The big money's on the dissolutions and buyouts, you know that. Three Dub wouldn't offer me a partnership until I proved I could run with the big boys." It felt good to be able to tell the truth. "The profits are quick, but those deals are just cookie-cutter. The challenge is making lemonade out of lemons." Alec fought to rein in his excitement before he sounded like Sunday.

"I can see. Show me what you're thinking."

They brainstormed ideas, and Alec ran through more spreadsheets, tweaking figures and forecasting income streams. They sat shoulder-to-shoulder on the towel, and Alec wasn't sure which was more of a turn-on, the possibility of a new deal, or the way Brant shared his enthusiasm.

"So, you haven't really said yes or no," Brant said.

"To which question, because it feels like we've both been saying 'Yes' an awful lot lately." Alec grinned and shot Brant a sizzling glance.

"You're right. I've only been thinking of asking."

Alec waited, his pulse drowning out the sound of the surf. What would Brant ask?

"Would you consider a job helping me turn Turner around? I suspect your days at Three Dub are numbered anyway."

"Maybe not. The way I'm seeing this, you are making the acquisition. So . . ."

"The Dubs aren't going to be thrilled if I keep Turner and don't sell off the pieces; they'll lose out on the most lucrative part of the original deal, the dissolution."

"I think I'd rather have you break that to them—" His words were cut off by a high-pitched wailing in the distance. Sunday!

"Uncle B, helllllp," Sunday screamed.

CHAPTER THIRTEEN

Brant's heart pounded. What had happened? He jumped up and raced toward her, in the distance. The soft sand impeded his steps and even with the cool ocean breeze, heat and humidity made every step take the effort of two or three. He saw her up ahead, near the waterline leaning over something on the sand–*Jenner.*

"What happened," Brant shouted as he neared her.

"I d-don't know. We were trying to see who could stay under longest and he won. Then when we were walking back to you, he suddenly said 'Ow,' then he fell down and-and . . . Help him!"

Brant's medical training kicked in. He felt for pulse, checked for breathing. Alec had caught up to them and stood back a few paces, holding onto a sobbing Sunday, watching.

"His pulse is very weak and he's barely breathing. There's a red welt on his arm, probably from a bite or a sting. Sunday, tell me what he touched and where. Show Alec where it is, but don't touch it."

"I'm s-sorry. I'm sorry!" she kept chanting.

Alec knelt down in front of her and took hold of her shoulders. "Sunday, Jenner is going to be fine, if you just help us figure out what happened."

She gulped air and sobbed, but nodded. "I dared him to touch this really gross thing. A squid or jellyfish or something. Over back there." She pointed farther up the beach. Alec raced over to look at it, while Brant continued to monitor Jenner's vital signs.

"We've got to get him to a hospital. There's bound to be an antivenin for whatever stung him," Brant said, loud enough for Alec to hear. "Can you tell what it is?"

"Jellyfish, I think. It's got these long . . . things."

"Well, stay far back from it. It's either not dead or the venom is on the surface."

"Uncle B, help him," Sunday mumbled through tears.

"Lemme call your mom." He felt around in his pocket. No phone. Ellie had taken it away from him. "Fuck!"

Alec was back at his side now. "The wind is low now, it will take ages to get back around the island. Can we make it to the road from here?"

Brant shook his head. "Not in time." Suddenly the idyllic secret beach, accessible only from the sea, was a nightmare.

On the sand in front of him, Jenner began gasping.

"The venom is moving through his body. He needs air." Brant checked Jenner's mouth and throat. "His throat's closing. Soon he won't be able to breathe at all."

"Sunday, can you run really fast to the road and get to a phone to call your mom at the hospital? Has she been here before?"

"Yes, she knows this beach."

"Tell her about the jellyfish and . . ."

Sunday had already taken off running.

Jenner's breathing was labored and even mouth-to-mouth was practically useless.

"Can't you, you know, do the thing where you open his throat up?" Alec asked.

Brant's stomach tightened into harder knots. He knew that's what Jenner needed, but *could he?* The last time had been on Voight.

"Yeah. I'll need...," he rattled off the items, and Alec ran to their backpacks to retrieve them while Brant focused on Jenner.

He had to remember he was the only one who could save him in time. No matter what had happened in the past, this was Jenner, his nephew. His own flesh and blood!

Alec returned with arms full. He spread out the picnic blanket and they eased Jenner onto it. Then Brant used a lighter to sterilize Alec's penknife, gathered up the napkins, and poured some alcohol from the first-aid kit onto Jenner's throat. He felt around for the correct spot and held the point of the blade against Jenner's throat while he calmed his frazzled nerves.

Deep breath.

Alec sat facing him, ready to mop up the blood with the napkins.

"What's wrong?" Alec's tone was a mix of worry and impatience.

Brant poised the blade again. "I-I-God, I haven't done something like this for years." Everything he'd felt when Byron Voight had nearly died bubbled to the surface, and every nerve was raw and aching.

"You've got the training, Brant. It'll come back. Just like riding a bike." Alec's tone was reassuring but firm.

Brant glared at Alec. You can't kill someone by falling off your bike.

"I know you can do this, Brant. Jenner needs you now." Alec laid a hand on Brant's arm, a warm, trusting, reassuring gesture that focused Brant's scattered thoughts.

Alec was right. What was wrong with Brant? Jenner made a strangled sound; his airway was now completely blocked. Without a thought Brant grasped the knife and cut.

He allowed instinct and training to take over. His hands worked, mouth issued directions to Alec as if on auto-pilot. Then Brant heard Jenner's breath, strong and clear, in and out, in and out, through the pen.

"That was amazing!"

"No, it wasn't." Now that his instinctual reactions had shut down and conscious thought processes had returned, Brant felt sick.

"Yeah, it was. He's breathing okay now."

It hadn't been pretty, but Brant had gotten Jenner breathing again. He still needed the antivenin. Alec had seen Brant choke during the emergency, but for now he wasn't letting it show—if he'd lost respect for Brant . . . He fought to keep the tears back.

Alec moved next to Brant on the sand and put an arm around him. Without a single word, he simply held on, squeezing Brant close, offering support, but as much as Brant wanted and needed it, he knew he had to hang on to his composure until Jenner was safe.

The sound of a helicopter approaching caught Brant's attention, and he met Alec's gaze, hoping to convey the gratitude he felt. He turned again to Jenner and smoothed the damp hair from the boy's face. He watched Jenner's chest rise and fall in shallow, jagged breaths.

In and out. In and out.

In a daze, Brant watched the 'copter land far enough down the beach to avoid flinging sand onto the injured boy. Ellie and a man— probably an EMT—hopped out before it touched down and ran toward Jenner. Alec led the man in the direction of the jellyfish, while Ellie stayed with Jenner and Brant. She checked his vitals with the proper equipment as her companion shouted which antivenin to use. Ellie pulled the vial from the case and injected the fluid into Jenner's arm while Brant watched.

"Thank God you were with him," Ellie said, and then she also broke into tears.

Brant went in the helicopter with Jenner, after Alec insisted he and Sunday could sail home. Later, Alec explained she'd been too afraid of leaving with Ellie, since she still felt the whole thing had been her fault for daring Jenner to touch the jellyfish in the first place.

That evening they all sat around Jenner's bed in the hospital. Even though he was fine, Ellie insisted he stay overnight for observation, with the five of them sleeping fitfully in the waiting room. The next morning, Jenner seemed eager to get home, but he asked Brant to retell the story of the operation over and over, until Ellie forced him to go to bed.

"Brant, I need to talk to you for a minute. In private." Ellie came in from the kitchen and set down a tray of coffee for the adults, but her tone told Brant there was trouble. He followed her back into the kitchen, glancing back at Alec whose worried look set the butterflies stirring in Brant's gut again.

"What is it?"

"When we got back I happened to notice a message on your phone. A text came in while we were at the hospital. I only looked because it said 'URGENT'"

Brant frowned. His assistant would have called Ellie's home number if she couldn't get him on the cell or email. "OK, thanks for letting me know. I'll take care of it now."

"Yes, you will. Right now."

"I don't understand. Where's the phone?"

"The problem is here. Or rather isn't here. The message was from 'AK' and said he loves you and wants to fix things with you."

It began to sink in. Brant's stomach threatened to bring up the coffee he'd just drunk, and he glanced away from Ellie.

"Yeah, well, I, uh...."

"Nice job. If your boyfriend 'AK' is texting you from New York, who the hell is in my living room?"

CHAPTER FOURTEEN

"Alec is . . ."

"Alec, AK. I brushed it off as a nickname. But Alec's not the boyfriend you mentioned before, is he?"

"No, not exactly."

"Well, what *exactly* is he? And what did he have to do with Jenner getting hurt?" Ellie's voice became territorial on top of angry. "Don't you dare tell me you hired some *hooker* to pose as your boyfriend and had the gall to introduce him to my kids then fuck him in my house!"

"No." Brant started to laugh off her outrageous scenario, but the vein throbbing in her forehead stopped his mirth in its tracks. "No. He showed up to finalized a deal with me and—"

"That's the 'unfinished business' he mentioned? This is all about a *business* deal?"

Ellie's voice hit a new high in pitch and intensity. She seemed angrier about the deal than about Brant fucking a hooker under her roof. "Is that what you two were doing while

Jenner got hurt? Talking *business?*" Ellie shot a withering glance toward the other room where Alec and Henri were having coffee, then back at Brant. Her eyes were half-closed but her gaze shot daggers right through every layer of Brant's skin.

"I know I should have been watching them more closely at the beach. But they stayed within sight." Brant paused. "Then I guess we got caught up talking business and…. As for Alec, I actually never—" Brant stopped short, knowing nothing he could say would be an acceptable excuse for what happened.

"You never what? Sunday Brant Linton, you tell me the truth right now. My son almost died because you were too distracted with business to watch him!"

"Well, it's not—"

"That's it. I'm done with your lies and I'm done with you. You're the actor. I didn't even figure it out because you two looked like a couple in love. No wonder you're so successful at what you do. Now I understand how you conned so many companies into selling out, when all the while you were planning to destroy their businesses and sell off the pieces to line your own pockets."

Ellie always had a knack for knowing Brant better than he knew himself sometimes. There had been more deception over the years than he cared to admit, but he'd never forced anyone to sign away anything.

"Your opinion of my business methods isn't important right now. Jenner is."

"You're right. Family comes first. As pissed off as I am with you right now, you did save Jenner's life, so I won't toss you out on your ear just yet. But Alec—or whatever his name is—doesn't belong here with us, not now. He's not family, and he's not even your boyfriend." She turned on her heel and slammed the kitchen door open, heading for the living room faster than Brant expected.

"Alec, Brant just admitted to the charade you've been playing. Coming here pretending to be his boyfriend just to get around my no-business rule. Well, your business here is finished. I'd like you to leave."

Brant chest ached as he watched Alec's smile crumble away in disbelief.

Henri stared at her, "*Chérie*, what's all this about?"

She summed up the details, all the while shooting daggers at both Alec and Brant.

"Come on, Ellie. This isn't necessary. It's not Alec's fault.' Brant put a hand on Ellie's shoulder.

"Get packing." She moved out of Brant's reach, then folded her arms across her chest and stared at Alec.

He glanced at Brant, then nodded. "Ellie, I completely understand why you're upset, and I'm really sorry I deceived you." Alec kept his voice even, though the pain in his eyes was obvious.

"Don't call me 'Ellie.' It's 'Eleanor' to you now!"

"I'm going, too," Brant said, but Ellie grabbed his arm.

"Brant, you stay. As mad as I am at you, the kids would be heartbroken if you left. Jenner's in the hospital and if you leave, it could set back his recovery. I won't let you do any more harm to him. But Alec, he's another matter."

Alec went upstairs without further comment, and Ellie huffed back into the kitchen with Henri following behind murmuring soothing sounds in French.

Brant followed Alec, torn between him and what Ellie had said about Jenner. Alec seemed surprised when Brant shut the door.

"Your sister is right, Brant. We lied and now we're paying for it. But you need to stay. I don't mind leaving, and I would never get between you and your family. I guess I got too comfortable with you and forgot where to draw the line between business and personal." He tossed his suitcase on the bed and started packing.

"Shut up, Alec. You know this is more than business. I'd gladly give up the damn deal, but I won't let you suffer those consequences, too." He took Alec's then pulled him close. "I thought *we were* real. Am I wrong, too?"

"No." Alec exhaled warmth against the back of Brant's neck and Brant felt a tiny shiver of arousal. He forced it away, but Alec felt so good in his arms. Felt like he belonged here. Alec was a good person; he'd changed Brant's mind about Turner Foods, about how he approached business. No one had had such a positive effect on him before, not even Voight. Ellie couldn't see it right now, but Brant would make sure she did before he left.

"Let me talk to Ellie. I'm sure she'll come around."

Alec stepped out of Brant's arms and it felt like the temperature dropped fifty degrees.

"Not like this. She'll resent me if you talk her into changing her mind. But I appreciate your gallantry." Then he moved in for a quick kiss before turning back to packing.

Brant pulled his emotions under control. He understood even if he didn't agree with Alec's choice. "As soon as Jenner's out of danger, I'll leave. A day or two at most. Wait for me on Raiatea or—"

"No. Let me fly back to New York and get these contracts amended. Assuming you still want to do this deal, the new deal."

"Yes. I love the idea of running the company. It will be something new. Something good. I haven't challenged myself much lately, at least, until I met you."

"Maybe I'm too much of a challenge?" Alec's unexpectedly flirty tone boosted Brant's spirits a notch. It wasn't how he'd envisioned the end of their trip, but thankfully Alec wasn't going to let it affect their relationship. There would be time to make this up to him.

"You're just the right amount of challenge for me, Alec." Brant loved that Alec had continually surprised him, forced him to reexamine himself and his choices. "Ellie, on the other hand, is too much for me." As soon as the words left his mouth, Brant burst into laughter. "All my life I've been trying to catch up with her, pass her. But just this minute I realized I never really will. And you know what? I never felt better." He paused. "Not about you leaving, I mean."

"I know what you meant, and I'm glad. Competition can go too far. Look at Jenner and Sunday."

"Yeah." Brant's thoughts took a serious turn. "I feel responsible for that too, telling them all those stories about me trying to outdo Ellie. Maybe that's what intensified their little war to a new level."

Brant carried Alec's suitcase downstairs where Ellie waited with arms still folded across her chest. Henri gave a disappointed shrug, but Brant didn't blame him that he couldn't get Ellie to budge on her decision.

"I'll drive Alec to the ferry. Can we take your car?" Brant asked.

"I've called a cab." Ellie's voice and eyes were hard. "It's already waiting outside."

"That's quick."

"Sorry to have you leave like this, Alec," Henri said. "It was a great Christmas, no matter how it all ended up." He held out his hand to Alec and they shook warmly. Henri pulled him in and whispered something into Alec's ear, but Brant couldn't hear.

"Thank you for letting me into your family for a little while." Alec hovered in the doorway, despite Ellie throwing him "hurry up already" looks and a few glances in the direction of Sunday's bedroom upstairs. "I won't forget this trip for a long time. Will you say goodbye to the kids for me?"

"Sure." Ellie glanced away, and Brant thought he detected a flicker of embarrassment in her gaze.

"I'll wait with you until the next ferry."

"I'd rather not. I'll see you in New York in a few days, and we'll continue work on how to fix Turner Foods' problems then. Who knows, maybe I'll figure out everything myself and scoop you on the deal."

Alec laughed but Brant saw through the act and followed him to the cab.

"You're not really leaving now, are you? Without a flight?"

"Yes. And you need to stay and sort things out with your family. I'll go back to Bora Bora and take the first flight out, wherever it's going."

"You don't let anything set you back."

"Nope." Alec treated Brant to the cocky grin he'd gotten used to already. "Talk to Ellie. The deal—and I—will be waiting when you get back."

Brant nodded, heart aching. He embraced Alec one last time and kissed him hard enough he'd remember it for the next few days, ignoring Ellie's gaze burning into the back of his head from the doorway.

Alec gave him a final squeeze, then got into the cab and disappeared from view.

Brant stood watching the cab for a few minutes before finally turning and heading back inside. The only relief was hope he could patch things up with Ellie, then go home to Alec with a smoother road ahead for them.

"This really was the best Christmas yet, until Jenner got hurt." Brant sat on a chair facing Henri and Ellie on the couch. "Alec helped me save his life. If he hadn't been there, I'm not sure I could have done it."

"Well, if Alec hadn't been there, Jenner probably wouldn't have gotten hurt in the first place. You'd have given the twins your full concentration, and he'd never have wandered out of your sight."

"Ellie, *chérie*, children wander off. Even with us. How many times have we let them out to play on their own? We cannot watch them twenty-four hours a day. You should not blame Alec or Brant for this. It was an unfortunate accident."

"No, Henri, Ellie's right. And it's also my fault Sunday dared Jenner into touching the jellyfish in the first place."

"What do you mean *dared?*" Ellie sat up, tense again.

"They heard us talking, how we used to try to outdo each other all the time. How I hated being the little brother, and I always wanted to do something bigger and better than you. I hadn't realized how much of our rivalry they understood."

She frowned for a moment and shook her head. "I never imagined it could get out of hand. But kids take things to heart in ways we can't predict. But Henri's right. I shouldn't blame you for Jenner." She exhaled loudly. "But I do blame you for lying about Alec."

Now they were getting somewhere. To Brant's surprise, Ellie was still more upset about this than Jenner's accident.

"Alec didn't tell you he was AK, did he?"

"No, but he didn't say he wasn't. He let me keep thinking he was your boyfriend. And you let me keep thinking so, too. And all the time two were alone you were doing some stupid deal?"

"Well, not all the time." Brant felt heat creep up his neck and burn the tops of his ears.

"Those kisses looked genuine to me, *chérie*." Henri chuckled and Ellie turned her angry gaze him.

"Well, Alec knows how to take a lie and sell it, even going *there*."

"I really like Alec. I just didn't get to know him until he was here. The sparks between us were a surprise but not at all unwelcome."

"Was there ever an AK?"

"Yes, AK was real. Is real. I'm not seeing him anymore. We weren't a good fit." Brant explained about why things hadn't worked out. By the end of the story, Ellie was laughing at Brant's discovery of a nearly empty apartment. "I found Alec so attractive when I first met him because part of me had already finished with AK. But it wasn't until he talked me out of the deal he'd come here to push I knew something deeper was possible. Something real and worth pursuing."

"Talked you out of it? Sounded like you're still doing it. The deal, I mean," Ellie blushed a bit at her unintended double entendre.

"We're doing a different deal. Instead of buying and stripping Turner Foods, Alec talked me into keeping the company. They need some operational fixes no one's been willing to try. I can afford temporary losses while trying to turn the company around. There's a whole new generation that doesn't appreciate Turner Foods yet, and maybe we can change that."

"Yeah, it would be a shame to see it disappear. I've got my own favorite Turner products. There's even a box of Crispy Pops I've got in the back of the cupboard. Don't tell Henri, though." She threw her husband a guilty look.

Brant hoped Ellie wouldn't notice the box was empty until he'd gone.

"That's the point Alec made, and I agree. It's too easy to look at a company as a set of figures and forget there's a face and a name and a story behind every person who works there. It's more of a challenge to fix the problems than to break apart and sell the pieces. And you know how much I like a challenge. I want Alec's advice going forward.

Besides, he'll probably need a new job when he gets back. His boss told him to finalize the dissolution with me or he'd get fired. That's why he followed me here in the first place."

"And he still tried to talk you out of the deal?" Henri asked.

Brant nodded.

Ellie chewed on her lower lip. "Maybe I overreacted."

"Ya think?" Henri asked with such a deadpan face and perfect American accent even Ellie burst into laughter.

"Why's everyone still up? Is Jenner okay?" Sunday came down the stairs, pausing between steps and rubbing sleep out of her eyes.

"Yes, honey, he's fine. Come here." Ellie held her arms out and Sunday settled onto her lap.

"Where's Alec?" Sunday looked around, her voice small and still full of worry.

"He's—" Brant started but Ellie held up a hand to silence him.

"He went for a walk, but he's been gone an awfully long time. Maybe Uncle Brant should take the car and look for him."

Henri's mouth fell open, and Ellie glared at him, then smiled.

Brant didn't need to be told twice. He leapt up, grabbed the car keys from the hook near the door, and went after Alec.

He found him in the harbor waiting room. The next ferry was still hours away, and he sat on his own, reading yesterday's discarded newspaper. He looked up as Brant approached.

"Did you get thrown out, too?" Alec grinned, no trace of irony or anger in his voice.

"Ellie admits she overreacted. I think she would have come herself, but Sunday woke up and she's getting her back to bed. If you don't want to come back, after the way she treated you, I wouldn't hold it against you."

"What would you hold against me?" Alec asked in a passable Mae West impersonation.

"Anything you like." Brant couldn't believe how calmly Alec was taking the whole situation and his respect grew even deeper. Alec hadn't argued or blamed anyone else. That was probably how he'd been so successful so far on Wall Street. He rolled with the punches, dealt with the situation at hand, and when he couldn't do anything, he backed off.

Perhaps Three Dub wouldn't let him go after all. There couldn't be many like Alec Compton on their payroll and they'd be fools to replace him with the kind of hard-working but mediocre toady who filled the ranks at most Wall Street firms.

"Ellie certainly owes you an apology."

"I'd settle for breakfast in bed, maybe pancakes with mango marmalade . . . Think she'd give me a foot massage?"

"No, but I will. Only I won't stop with your feet." Brant threw his arms around Alec and kissed him hard, then whispered what else he intended into Alec's ear, even though they were alone.

"And that would definitely be the best Christmas bonus I've ever gotten."

THE END

Word of mouth is extremely important for independent authors. So if you enjoyed this book, please leave a review at Amazon or recommend it to a friend. Thank you.

EM Lynley

About the Author

EM Lynley writes gay erotic romance. She loves books where the hero gets the guy and the loving is 11 on a scale of 10. A Rainbow Award winner and EPIC finalist, EM has worked in high finance, high tech, and in the wine industry, though she'd rather be writing hot, romantic man-on-man action. She spent 10 years as an economist and financial analyst, including a year as a White House Staff Economist, but only because all the intern positions were filled. Tired of boring herself and others with dry business reports and articles, her creative muse is back and naughtier than ever. She has lived and worked in London, Tokyo and Washington, D.C., but the San Francisco Bay Area is home for now.

She is the author of *Sex, Lies & Wedding Bells*, the Precious Gems series from Dreamspinner Press, and the Rewriting History series starring a sexy jewel thief, among others.

Visit her online:
Website: http://www.emlynley.com/

Blog: http://www.emlynley.com/blog

Free Reads:
http://www.emlynley.com/free-stories/

Facebook
https://www.facebook.com/emlynley

Twitter
https://twitter.com/emlynley

Newsletter
http://www.emlynley.com/about-contact/newsletter/

OTHER TITLES BY EM LYNLEY

Available at Amazon and other book distributors.

Visit My Amazon Author Page:
http://bit.ly/amz-eml2

NOVELS
Bound for Trouble
Out of the Gate
Spaghetti Western
Jaded
An Intoxicating Crush
Lighting the Way Home
Hostile Takeover
Italian Ice
Rarer Than Rubies
Dirty Dining (forthcoming January 2015)
Sex, Lies & Wedding Bells (2nd edition, forthcoming March 2015)

NOVELLAS
Irresistible Forces (in *Unconditional Surrender* Box Set)
Gingerbread Palace
Snow Job – 2013 LRC New Adult Book of the Year
Venus Envy
A Lesser Evil
Brand New Flavor
A Christmas Bonus

NON-FICTION
How to Be a NaNoWriMo Winner
Tax Tips for Authors 2014
How to Revise Your NaNoWriMo Novel (forthcoming Jan 2015)

EDITOR
Bedknobs & Beanstalks
Going for Gold Olympic Anthology
Wicked Good
Rumpled Silk Sheets

COPYRIGHT

www.ingramcontent.com/pod-product-compliance
Lightning Source LLC
Chambersburg PA
CBHW060926120626
46557CB00003B/893